Adrian Mitchell was born in London in 1932. He spent his time at Oxford writing, and left without a degree. He adapted Jose Triana's play, *The Criminals*, and Peter Weiss' *Marat/Sade* for the Royal Shakespeare Company. He also wrote the lyrics for Peter Brook's *US*, and his play, *Tyger*, was performed by the National Theatre Company. He has published three books of poems, *Poems* (1964), *Out Loud* (1968), and *Ride the Nightmare* (1971). His novel, *The Bodyguard* (1970) is published in Picador. Since 1959, he has read his poems all over Britain, as well as in Belgium, Cuba, France and America.

Also by Adrian Mitchell in Picador

The Bodyguard

Adrian Mitchell

Wartime

PICADOR
Published by Pan Books Limited

First published 1973 by Jonathan Cape Limited
This Picador edition published 1975 by
Pan Books Limited, Cavaye Place, London SW10 9PG

ISBN 0 330 24467 1

Made and printed in Great Britain by
Richard Clay (The Chaucer Press) Ltd, Bungay, Suffolk

Contents

Beginning

1953

He was alive. His flesh shifted continuously on the old bone-frame. But Colonel Munche was imagining himself dead. His head, a worn, heavy wedge, nodded. His bullet eyes were hidden. He saw his own corpse.

Slumped, right hand jammed in the Luger drawer of his desk, wet brains drying on the blotter, the green, thirsty blotter. Blotted clots. Half-decapitated on the black settee, his Adam's apple halved by a kukri. Staggering eccentrically, hand to throat, across the carpeted acres of a regimental reception, attempting and failing to vomit, face wrenched into hard yellow lines, arsenic spilling from his whisky glass. His body efficiently crucified to the holy turf of Lords by three cricket stumps. A heap of waste matter, gutty litter, at the foot of the white cliffs of somewhere, hook-beaked, un-English birds spiralling down for lunch. Drowned, in a plastic washing-up bowl stained brown with old tea, by an Oriental wrestling champion. How had his wife dared bring such a bowl into the house; it was disgusting when she bought it but now it was the embodiment of scuffed grubbiness. He would destroy it, bury it if he couldn't burn it. A bad bowl doomed. Ha.

Colonel Munche was sweating, partly with the heat of the afternoon. He began to count up to his own age, fifty-seven, fifty-eight, fifty-nine, sixty, sixty-one. His soft-stepping, bowl-buying wife appeared beside him. The Colonel jerked as he realized she was there. Her bones were light.

'Poached egg and spinach for lunch, dear?'

'Delightful,' sarcastically. 'But what am I to eat for my lunch?'

'Poached egg and spinach, dear.'

'You came in here to tell me that?'

His voice became as gentle as hers, though much calmer. He didn't want her in the room.

'I'm sorry dear, I thought you liked to be told the—'

In her fear, she couldn't remember the right word for two staring seconds. He waited.

'—the menu.'

'I don't like being interrupted. I hate being suddenly interrupted, especially quietly, I was thinking hard about important things. Very important – if you want to know the truth, I was thinking about death. When I want to think hard about something as important as death I come to my study. I expect the courtesy of a knock on the door. With the back of your knuckles like this—' he rapped on his desk until it hurt, 'the courtesy of a knock. I don't suppose you understand, I don't suppose you spend much time thinking about important things like death. But you are right about just one thing. I do like to know the menu so that I can prepare for it. Eggs and spinach. Are you going to tell me that spinach contains iron?'

'It does, you know. So good for you.'

'I know that spinach contains iron. I have an excellent encyclopaedia of vegetables with seven pages about spinach together with a coloured illustration. I received a thorough and expensive education which included enormous quantities of spinach. I know about iron. Spinach tastes of iron. As if I needed iron. At my age. What would I use it for? I shan't be growing any more, thank you. I'm quite big enough, thank you. Think of something else.'

'You don't want poached eggs, even without spinach, dear?'

'I'd rather chew the meat off your skinny shoulder-blades.'

He laughed.

'Now tell me what we're having for lunch.'

He stood up. His body was tall and thick, arms heavy. He stood in front of her. In his shadow, she sucked in her pale cheeks.

'Sardine salad?'

'Say that again.'

'Sardine salad, dear?'

'Say that once more.'

Still smiling, he raised his right hand, half-clenching it.

'Tinned crab and boiled potatoes?'

'Tinned crab and boiled potatoes.'

He came close. Her high voice soared.

'Chops and cabbage and boiled potatoes. Spaghetti and salad. Rabbit curry. Curry. Curry.'

He took those delicate shoulders in his hands. His heavy fingers typed a message on her back. Their foreheads bumped and then bumped again and the bumping continued. The impact did not hurt him as the front of his skull collided with the yellowed bruise on her brow. His brain was a dark purple parade-ground on which the numbers appeared in scarlet – one for the spinach, two for the bowl, three for the interruption, four for the boiled potatoes, five for the wasted years – as their heads met. In her wincing brain, two inches away from his, she recited to herself the almost hopeless spell: if I had money of my own I could go to Bath and live there for ever with Dorothy. But I can't even draw a pension yet. I can't work, I really do not see how I could work, even a nice job in Bath. Bath is a spa. The Romans liked it.

Six months before she had dared to tell Dorothy, over the stainless steel teapot on the fourth floor of Blooter's, the Belston department store: 'Yes dear, I'm sure you're right, you are so wise, Dorothy. Of course I should leave the Colonel now Mummy's gone. But Dorothy, what would I do? No dear, I know you can't afford to pay for my food, even though I do seem to be eating less and less. I was never trained for anything except hockey and lax and I was always too skinny, oh yes Dorothy I was, for either of those. I'm sure sheepdogs are trained more thoroughly than I was. Have you ever been to the *Daily Express* Sheepdog Trials? No, nor have I, but I should like to go. Of course, I should come back with you to Bath and address envelopes for charity or something, but charity doesn't pay very well, does it? And I'm sure I should lose jobs and tell my landlady exactly what I thought of her. Well, I should really have to tell her. I'm like that, you know, Dorothy, I'm really outspoken underneath. And I'm really so much better at suffering than work, perhaps suffering's my talent, we all do have a talent, don't we Dorothy? And the Colonel can be quite sweet when he wants to be. He has such a sense of humour, which of course I haven't got. A woman can do without a sense of humour. I think so. But I don't regret. So much luckier than so many people, I expect.'

Dorothy had almost lost her temper. She had travelled second class from Bath to Belston and stayed in a private hotel with unemptied ashtrays, purely in order to rescue her weak friend from marriage to a dirty old sadist. A Colonel? There are no Colonels any more, or if there are they are mere clichés with no power at all, outdated Aunt Sallys for embittered lefties. Dorothy had read that in the papers, several times. But it wasn't that she hated Colonels, but she did hate this one. It is possible to believe the *Sunday Telegraph* and hate a Colonel. Be that as it is, Dorothy returned to Bath the same day.

The heavy fingers rested, splayed on Mrs Munche's back. They allowed her to retreat four little steps, then let her go. The Colonel laughed as something nudged his sense of humour. A Tory joke not worth recording.

As the thick door closed behind Mrs Munche, two heads appeared at the study window – the elongated head of the ex-cavalry horse Masterman and, just above it, the mouth-dominated head of the Colonel's only daughter, Lorna, voluminous yellow hair bundled into her riding cap. As usual, she wore field-glasses. At twenty-two she spent much of her time investigating the distance. She loved excitement. She loved her father, who gave her many things. His voice, for her sake, became tender.

'Hello, Pussy-willow,' he said.

She rocked herself in the saddle and smiled. Moist, he thought, I have a moist daughter.

'Three teenagers came over the West Wall ten minutes ago,' she said. 'Boys. With air-guns.'

'Did they see you?'

'Don't imagine so. I stalked them. They were heading for our woods.'

'After my rabbits. Wait for me. Wait. We'll catch them, haul them in. Like fishes, into the net, up into the dry air, watch 'em writhe. You take Masterman through the West Meadow. When you get between the boys and the fence, flush 'em out the other side of the wood. You've got your crop? Good. I'll cycle up the bridle path and catch them as you chase them out. Teach them a lesson.'

'What if they split up? Three of them.'

'We'll catch one and teach him a lesson he can pass on to his little chums.'

'They're not that little.'

'Never too old for a lesson.'

Lorna nodded, accustomed to her father's delightful miniature campaigns. He loaded his shot-gun with hardly a glance at it, slung its webbing strap over his shoulder and strode out to his one-speed bicycle.

Colonel Munche did some gentle things in his life as well as many cruel things. But he was more taken by cruelty. He may have dominated these early pages, but he will not dominate this book. He will make his exit before long.

Jack knew the Munche Woods. He led Rodney and Mike down a path which had been scribbled all over by brambles and nettles. They snapped through a brittle bush into an oval clearing.

Rodney said: 'Don't see any rabbits.'

Mike said: 'You have to wait.'

They tried to wait. As they crouched on the dried earth, Jack began to chant in a concentrated croon:

'Coney, coney, I love you.
Come and be my rabbit stew.
You shall live on ha'penny carrots
In the burrow of my guts.
Coney, coney, I love you,
Come and be my rabbit stew.'

A rabbit bounced slowly into the open. It either saw Rodney's reaction or heard the violent breath before he raised his gun. It gave a sideways hop out of the oval. Mike laughed.

'That's no good. That's not waiting. Gently. Wait.'

They let the next rabbit, or it might have been the same one, reach the exact centre of the bare earth before firing – three pellets in the same second. As the rabbit responded to the noise with a leap, two pellets hit. It jerked, rolled, jerked and then stopped jerking. As Mike picked it up they heard sticks crack and a horse at their backs.

'Out this way,' said Jack, as they began to run.

'What if the old Colonel catches us?' said Rodney. 'Do we split up?'

'Stick together,' said Mike. 'Better to stick together.'

Jack agreed. 'He's a bloody king of devils. Stay together. Nothing much he can do to all three of us at the same time.'

The horse behind them seemed in no hurry; perhaps they hadn't been heard. As they broke out of the wood they slowed to catch their breath. There was a wordless shout. Astride his bicycle stood the Colonel, shot-gun at his shoulder, pointing at them. The bike made him uncomfortable; it was awkward physically to stand with the machine between one's legs, awkward and vaguely unworthy. Bicycles are not serious machines. But he looked sufficiently frightening to the boys.

'Run!' said Rodney.

'Stop!' shouted the Colonel. 'Stop, you little swine, or I'll shoot you down like swine.'

'Better stop,' said Mike.

Jack hadn't even started. His head was back and he laughed. His forefinger, shaking, pointed back at the Colonel's gun.

'The cad shoots pigs. Pigs should be stuck. And you stick them from a pony, not from a one-speed 1949 BSA with a battery headlamp. Swine is pigs,' he said, turning to Rodney. 'Like cattle is kine, pigs is swine—'

Rodney: 'Shut up.'

Mike put his hand on Jack's shoulder. They watched the Colonel walk towards them, still astride his bike.

'After my rabbits, after my rabbits,' he muttered at them, concentrating his anger on their crime. Lorna on Masterman appeared behind them, cap tilted back, one hand on the reins, the other on her riding crop. Rodney was more scared of the horse than the Colonel's gun. Its teeth were enormous and yellow. It had bad breath. Death between the teeth of a horse would be a bloody tearing. Rodney looked at Lorna. She was as magnificent and terrible as her horse. He looked away and blinked to wipe her picture out of his eyes. Jack looked at Lorna and she was so obviously beautiful that he said the word 'beautiful' to himself. He grinned and quietly recited:

'Coney, coney, I love you.
Come and be my rabbit stew.
You shall live on ha'penny carrots
In the burrow of my guts.
Coney, coney, I love you,
Come and be my rabbit stew.'

Mike was impressed by Lorna, but he didn't like the look of her. He fixed his lips in a sour, tough smile. He observed the grass. A bad end, he remembered someone saying, she came to a bad end.

The Colonel snatched the rabbit from Mike and tied it to his bike with a short length of green garden twine. It swung from the handlebars.

'Back to the Hall, and I'll decide what we're going to do with you.'

Between the whirring bicycle, with long grass clicking against its spokes, and the brown smell of the horse, the three walked close to each other, holding their air-guns loosely. The weight of pellets in his pocket reminded Rodney of his guilt. He decided to be brave, so he spoke loudly:

'I'm sorry I got you two in a mess. It was my fault entirely. I suggested the whole thing.'

Mike was embarrassed by that; it was the kind of noble pronouncement he'd never heard spoken by a living person. Its tone was only familiar in school stories and Mike reckoned that school stories were full of shit.

'Don't be crazy; I mean, I like eating rabbits. Whoever they belong to. Anyhow, rabbits are wild, they don't belong to anyone.'

'Yes, well I like shooting them. There's the sport of it as well,' said Rodney nervously, then stopped, suddenly aware that he didn't understand a word he'd said.

'The rabbits like it too,' said Jack. 'They don't talk about it much, but they enjoy it. You can tell by the way they die.' He did a sudden impression of Bugs Bunny being shot with a huge and happy grin all over his face.

The Colonel's head swivelled.

'You'll be shooting no more rabbits on my land.'

Mike gave his dumbly insolent stare.

'Teach you a lesson,' said the Colonel.

Mike grinned and held the grin. The procession passed round the back of the Hall, watched by the ghost-trodden face of Mrs Munche. The Colonel and Lorna dismounted correctly before marching their prisoners into the house, past the heavy chest in the hall which held old uniforms, past the door which led down to the cellar, until they stood, like soldiers on a charge, before the desk. The Colonel sat down opposite them and held hands with himself. The shot-gun lay across the desk. Mentally Jack turned it into a blunderbuss, capable of firing nuts and bolts, like in *Beano*. Jack was seventeen and unemployed, lived on his own above a garage, but he still read *Beano*. He reckoned it was pretty accurate about life. The Colonel was straight out of *Beano*. Would he produce a yellow slipper to whack them with in the final frame, like the father in Dennis the Menace?

'Have to hand you over to the police. Let them deal with you.'

Rodney's mind ran straight to his father. It caught little comfort there. He knew his father to be easy-going – his father had often told him so, and Rodney had some proof. In company and in the local newspaper he edited, Barrett Brown preached that iron discipline had gone out with the Iron Duke and a good thing too. But if, in front of a town full of middle-aged men in suits with official positions, he were shown to be wrong, his son exposed as an unsuccessful poacher, would he change? Would he have the guts not to change? The most disturbing mystery in Rodney's life so far, and one of the reasons for the crowd of fears in his head, had been the way people changed, suddenly, unpredictably. He never changed much himself.

Mike knew that poaching was nothing serious, but he took cops seriously. His father had met policemen during two bitter strikes. As Mike rolled a pinch of cheap trouserleg between finger and thumb, he recalled true stories about the police. There are alleys in Belston and there are cells. Never be alone with a policeman. The worst bit is when they make you take off your shoes; go down with the first punch, roll in a ball, guard your head, guard your balls.

Lorna yawned and stretched like a dancer. She leaned against the wall beside the door.

The Colonel: 'You boys know perfectly well that I ought to hand you over to the Law. The police might save you from yourselves.'

Jack thought of a joke but didn't crack it. He thought about the seaside instead, sleeping in sand-dunes, a small fire, a big girl, one of his favourite thoughts. This time he cast a softened version of Lorna in the role of the Big Girl. Big Rich Girl she must be too.

'I certainly ought to let the police deal with you. I have some good friends in the Force.'

Mike realized that they wouldn't, for some reason, be given to the Colonel's friends in the Force. The Colonel was acting anger. Mike was pleased. A cop had cuffed him and winded him with his elbow because of a street-corner joke and had then offered him a cigarette. The Colonel might be a more straightforward enemy. There was only one of him. Colonel Munche fetched himself a large whisky from a Victorian hi-fi set, sipped three times and smiled. Everyone was uncertain.

'But I know boys. I've been a boy. Ha. What's more, I've commanded boys. Better boys than you, though I'm sure they didn't come from such good homes. Disgrace upon parents. Blot. But I know, I know you're not real delinquents, not really rotten. Just a bunch of jackanapeses out for some sport. Well, I'm a sportsman myself, and I'd like to give you another chance.'

It wasn't so much Jack's grin as his red hair which infuriated the Colonel. The boy looked at him like an Irishman.

'I'd belt the life out of you if I was – but I wouldn't do that, boys, I might regret that. I forget my strength.'

Lorna stroked a door panel. The Colonel gestured towards a hefty piece of furniture containing silver cups. Two of the smaller ones were for Public School boxing. The rest were for intimidation at Bridge.

'Cider?' he asked.

Rodney hoped wildly that they might drink the Colonel under the table and escape on his bicycle, possibly rescuing Lorna, whose sleepy eyes bewildered him. But she watched only the Colonel as vintage cider splashed and rose in three large tumblers. The boys drank.

'Now, as I said, I'm a sportsman, and I've got a sporting proposition to make. Are you sportsmen?'

Jack said: 'We shoot rabbits. I can cook. Stew. I get vegetables cheap down the market. You know the market in Belston? Just by the Odeon, there's a couple of green doors back of the Odeon that don't shut too well.'

The Colonel glanced at Lorna. She smiled, so he smiled.

'Oh, a sense of humour. I like a lad with a sense of humour. Within reason. Now I could confiscate your guns, and then you might not grin, but I don't want to spoil your fun, and they'd be no use to me. Toys.'

He lifted the shot-gun about three inches off the desk and replaced it heavily.

'Do you want to hear my proposition?'

Mike looked over the edge of his golden drink. It was stronger than normal cider, certainly stronger.

'We'll hear it.'

Jack said: 'Shoot.'

Rodney stopped himself giggling. He was good at stopping himself from doing things.

'Fill up their glasses, Lorna.'

She did so, without looking one of the boys in the eye. But her hand touched, briefly, the hands which held the glasses.

'It's a sort of game, really. Game I used to play here as a lad with my brother. Died at Anzio. In action. Yes. The game. Do you know the Gulleys?'

Jack thought he knew the place the Colonel meant, but shook his head.

'There's a narrow valley through our woods, shaped like a letter Y. Cuts through the woods. Sort of valley, sort of ravine you might call it. Deep and steep. Lots of rock. Some trees. From one end of the Y-shape to the other it's about three hundred yards, whichever fork you take. Game we used to play was this. We'd get a friend, someone. One of us would start from each of the three ends of the Y—' he drew the Y-shape on his desk with a whisky-dipped finger, 'each one with an air-gun. And then we'd stalk each other, you know. I expect you used to do something like that in Scouts, if you were Scouts. Stalking. You've seen it done in cowboy films, I'm sure. Of course we never used to hurt each other. Great fun, great fun. The whole idea was, you see, to stalk on until one of us was hit by a pellet. Just a flesh wound, a graze, slight flesh wound. Can't go far wrong with one of those little air-guns, eh? Toys. But it's a test of skill. Strategy. You need skill in stalking, skill in shooting and, above all, and this may surprise you, strategic skill. What about that? And a little courage, ha? Not much, just a little bravado.'

Mike saw the point. He gulped cider and misunderstood deliberately.

'Do you want each of us to stalk you in turn?'

'An affair of honour? No, that would hardly be fair. I know the country, ha, I own the country, ha. And I'm a team shot, a team shot. No, if you were interested in this little idea, I'd be referee. There's a little temple thing up on the hill, about fifty feet up, just above the junction of the Y-shape. I can see most of the Gulleys from there, even through the trees. I'll adjudicate, don't be afraid I won't be fair. I play no favourites. Oh no.'

He refilled his glass.

Mike asked: 'What happens if we don't want to play?'

'Of course you don't have to—'

'Let's play Old Maid, loser to be lashed to the mouth of a cannon,' said Jack very quietly. He was staring into the depths of the cider. It would be interesting to keep a goldfish in a bowl of cider. It might sing. A mermaid would be better. The right sort of mermaid for Jack would have shortish hair so that it wouldn't cover her breasts like in books. There's nothing much prettier than a mermaid's breasts.

'If we don't play,' said Rodney, slowly, because the cider was already numbing his tongue, 'you'd take away our guns? Take us to the police?'

'Come, come.'

The Colonel had run out of words. He filled their glasses. The cider was a slightly darker gold than the sunshine outside.

'There's a prize, too. A prize. I didn't tell you about the prize, did I?'

'Your daughter's hand?' said Jack, thinking of tournaments

and letting loose a cider-powered laugh and a subsidiary fart.

'Young scoundrel. My daughter, indeed. No, not my daughter. That's my daughter. Not her, no. I am talking about money. Some money. Yes. Three pounds for the winner.' Pause. 'A pound for both the losers. Not just one prize, you see. Everybody gets a prize.'

Mike: 'What do you get? For your prize?'

'I told you, I'll be referee. It would take me back, you know, take me back.'

'We can use that money,' said Rodney, addressing everybody. 'Five pounds between us, win or lose.'

'How do you win?' asked Jack.

Mike looked out of the window.

'First to draw blood, I suppose,' he said.

Rodney: 'When do we stop?'

Jack: 'You mean, when do we start?'

'No, when does the stalking stop? How do we know?'

'It all stops as soon as anyone gets hit,' said the Colonel.

Rodney, pink with cider, said:

'Are you scared, Mike? I'm not scared.'

'You've got no need to be scared. We're both better shots than you. You're not likely to be very maimed.'

The Colonel clasped his hands.

'The thing to remember,' he said, 'is not to aim for the head if you can possibly help it. Unless of course you're close enough and accurate enough to graze the cheek,' he added, fading out the words dubiously. Mike drew a fingernail along his cheek, then looked at the nail and prised the salty dirt from under it with a tooth. Rodney looked uncertain.

'I don't want to shoot Mike. Or Jack.'

'It's a game,' said the Colonel. 'Only a game.'

Rodney: 'All right.'

Jack nodded.

Mike: 'We'll play.'

The Colonel: 'I'll guide you. Follow me.'

All of them picked up their guns. From somewhere upstairs a dog barked sharply. The boys, slightly dizzied by the open air and tripping occasionally on rough ground, trailed behind the Colonel towards the east. Lorna, on Masterman, galloped past them as they wove their way among birch trees, then scrambled down a fifty-degree slope into the junction of the Gulleys.

'What are your names?' the Colonel asked tenderly.

They told him and he repeated them, their Christian names. So he'll know what to put on our graves in the Regimental Cemetery, thought Mike.

'Who's the best shot? Right then, Jack – you take the base of the Gulleys. Michael and Rodney, each of you take one branch of the Y – stop when you reach the end of your gulley. I'll be able to see you from the temple.'

He pointed up at a circle of white pillars topped by a cupola, the summit of a wedding cake.

'I'll fire my gun once, then you can start. I want you to take your time. Don't rush it. Don't fire wildly, not till you've aligned your sights. Stick to cover when you can. Keep your heads down. Keep quiet, no shouting to each other. Now, have you all got plenty of ammo?'

Rodney distributed pellets fairly.

'Good, now let's see you load. Good. Come on. Good. Any questions?'

He shook hands with each of them. Behind the Colonel's back, Mike tried to mime some message to the others. The Colonel turned to find Rodney shrugging his incomprehension.

'Ah ha, no alliances, no treaties, no pacts. Every man for himself. Right. Off you go.'

For a moment he stood at the junction of the Y, watching them making for their starting points, his big right hand raised in salutation.

The gulley was darkened to twilight by trees, a twilight broken by spotlights where the sun came through. Rodney walked quickly between two high banks. Along the base of the gulley there were no trees, it was like a dried river bed, undulating often, obscured by rocks the size of desks and books, a few broken parts from trees. When he looked back after the first twenty yards he could no longer see the others, only the Colonel, becoming smaller as he climbed towards the temple. Rodney wished they had been able to discuss the rules of the game in more detail, including how to win without getting hurt and a Red Cross briefing just in case. The obvious target was the bum, plenty of protective flesh and little bone. But it would be hard to hit; he couldn't imagine either Jack or Mike running away from him. Mike's courage and Jack's craziness would keep them advancing. Even if they did turn their backs, there was the danger of hitting the breakable spine. A pellet might break it, might not. He imagined himself running away, the pellet lodged in his spinal cord, the small lead slug shaped rather like a vase becoming the centre, the hub of a growing wheel of pus deep under the skin of his back. Rodney blinked. He decided to aim for their legs, low down, and from a good distance. Or perhaps he should shoot wide and leave the wounding to the others. No, why should he?

The Colonel sat on the temple's marble bench, eyes hidden behind black field-glasses. He raised his shot-gun and fired once. Masterman neighed, braked temporarily, then resumed his precise path through the trees above the Gulleys. Lorna's mouth was open.

Rodney tightened his belt, toted his air-gun and noted the rocks ahead. He'd need no cover at first, he could walk down the middle of the deserted street like Gary Cooper. It would be seventy yards before he was likely to sight Jack. Rodney began to walk, his gun warming itself under his right arm, loose pellets milling around in his pocket. Uncertain of the rules, he didn't know if he was allowed to climb along the bank, among the thick trees. It seemed unfair, so he confined himself to the dusty, stone-littered gulley floor. Mike was probably parallel to him, approaching Jack at about the same rate. Jack was unlucky; it was, in a way, two against one. Rodney prepared to drop back behind a low-growing tree. But there was still nobody ahead of him. He must aim low, at the legs. At the legs. For a moment Rodney recalled who he was stalking, then forgot again as he remembered that he was being stalked. To mislead anyone listening in the silence, he picked up a large stone and, turning, hurled it back along the gulley to the place where he'd been standing when the Colonel fired his starting gun.

Standing casually, feet apart, Mike just missed the stone with a quick shot as it somersaulted below him. As soon as he'd heard the Colonel's gun, Mike had padded up the slope and over its crest so that he could surprise Rodney from the rear. Strategy. Or was it tactics? But he certainly wasn't going to hit Rodney, he knew Rodney was scared, and he felt himself responsible for this absurd, underpaid battle. He'd been hit by pellets before; for him an air-gun wound was something known. He'd rather face a small-fry air-gun than an erratic but more powerful catapult.

Rodney dropped as he heard Mike's shot. Bad. Now he would certainly be attacked from each end of his gulley. As he wriggled behind a rock, he saw Mike run down the slope and drop into a knee-high, circular trench which formed a dusty basin in the gulley's base.

Looking out of this highly pregnable fortress, Mike saw the barrel of Rodney's gun sticking out beside a heavy, six-foot-square rock. A giant, brittle, sugar lump of a rock. Mike reloaded and shot and hit the exact centre of the cube. There was a miniature shower of stone dust. Rodney replied with a random, fairly close shot. Mike immediately knew that he'd made a bad mistake, strategy to cock already. He should have stayed at the top of the slope, dodging among the trees; he'd been tempted by this stupid trench. It had looked deeper and safer from the crest because of the shadows. But it was too damn shallow, a bloody paddling pool. Rodney might easily get his head. Mike's head felt like a Belisha beacon. He should have spat that cider into an aspidistra, like in films. Between his trench and Rodney's rock there was no cover, no way of advancing except through the trees on the slopes each side of them. If Mike could reach one of those slopes – but there was little point in advancing. Jack might appear behind Rodney at any moment and raise the siege. But if so, Rodney would be forced up one of the slopes. Then the trench would provide no cover whatsoever.

Rodney fired again, once more to the right of the trench.

Immediately he heard the shot, Mike rose and ran for the slope, half-falling over a wrist-thick root, hearing the snap of Rodney's reload, dropping behind the first tree. A pellet burrowed into the earth in front of him. Mike leaped to the shadow of a bigger tree, a fat, bent, balding statesmanlike structure of dead and dying wood. He had the advantage again. He decided on a show of power. His first shot clicked a chip from the top edge of Rodney's rock. Rodney hesitated, then leaned out to fire, but before he could press the trigger, another chip broke off the rock, only a foot from his hands. Mike was loading fast, he knew how, breaking the air-gun with his left hand, pressing in the pellet with the same hand, clicking back the barrel, aim, fire.

Rodney tried to copy Mike's speed, but the sleeve of his jacket stuck between the barrel and the breech; he dropped a pellet and giggled. His upper teeth gripped his lower lip, the skin of his face was as red as his lips. Twice he hit Mike's tree, twice he missed. Meanwhile Mike hit the rock six times, calm, confident of his cover. But, moving to the lower side of his tree for a surprise shot, Mike slipped, arse-downwards, right into the open. Instead of trying to scramble up again, he let himself go with gravity, rolling down the slope like a log – a hard target for Rodney.

With one arm and the butt of his gun, Mike stopped himself. He lay behind a rise in the ground, out of Rodney's sight, but nearer than before. He regained his breath and listened.

Rodney reloaded with sweat-wet fingers. He couldn't make up his mind where Mike's roll had ended. Rodney guessed and fired again.

Mike raised his head, and a blunt little pellet skimmed a small ditch along the top of his scalp. First it began to burn, then it started to bleed gently. When the blood began, the cut hardly hurt at all. A flesh wound, just what the Colonel ordered. Mike crooned ancient obscenities to himself.

Rodney, not knowing he had scored and won, fired again.

The sound enraged Mike. He aimed carefully at Rodney's arm and brushed his sleeve with the shot. He loaded and crawled forward, ignoring cover, then ran up the slope at an angle and crouched behind another tree, loaded and fired again, ran on, crouched, loaded again. He had run blind, blood trickling away into his collar, something to be explained to his mother later. He found himself with half his anger left, staring straight down the slope towards Rodney. Then he smiled.

Down the gulley towards Rodney marched Jack, his gun

tilted on his shoulder, shouting out in a parody of the Colonel's voice:

'Coney, coney, I love you.
Come and be my rabbit stew—'

Then he stopped. And fell. He brushed his ginger hair back and forth among the small leaves. Rodney, surrounded, had panicked. Confronted by Jack, who had stalked up Mike's empty gulley and back again, Rodney had raised his gun and fired. The pellet caught Jack in the left eye. They ran to Jack, then shouted for the Colonel. Jack was screaming at first, then just panting and swearing quietly but solidly.

Up in his wedding-cake temple, the Colonel, his game over, wiped his cock on a handkerchief and zipped up his trousers. He began to walk down the slope, carefully trembling, with more happiness than he was used to.

Mike turned to Rodney, without taking his hands away from Jack's shoulders.

'What the hell were you playing at? You got my head, and you got Jack.'

'Did I hit you?'

Mike lowered his head. A puddle of blood was drying in his hair.

'I'm sorry, Mike. It must have been a wild shot. I didn't know I hit you.'

'You hit me.'

'I'm sorry. It was supposed to be a game.'

Rodney produced a handkerchief – he always carried one – and dabbed Mike's head. The Colonel appeared behind them.

'Well played, lads. Real soldiers. What? Two of you hit? That's too bad. Come back to the Hall and we'll patch you up.'

Then he began to understand what had happened to Jack. Jack wouldn't take his hand away from his eye. Lorna galloped up to them, dismounted, took Jack's arm and led the horse and the boy towards the Hall. Rodney moved between Mike and Jack with a mouthful of apologies.

'We'll look after him,' said the Colonel. 'Lorna knows something, a thing or two in fact, about nursing. First-aid box, always have it handy.'

Jack began to laugh.

Mrs Munche met them in the entrance hall. Brightly, eyeing the blood, she said:

'Hello. And what have you boys been up to?'

'They've been shooting in the Gulleys, my dear. Shot each other too. Well, well. Stick a bandage on this one, Jane, then send him down to my study. And this one—' inclining his head towards Jack, 'well, he's not so good, not so good as he was. Lorna had better put him to bed in the Blue Room. You ring for Doctor Clewes.'

'The doctor?'

'You heard me. Ring for that blasted doctor. Yes. Clewes. Our doctor. Get him over.'

In the vast, lilac-tiled bathroom, Mrs Munche washed and bandaged Mike's hair while he felt conscious of too much dandruff. She asked no questions, even of herself. She thought about the doctor, the Colonel's best friend, and talked unceasingly:

'You should always be so careful with guns, always careful. I remember my father used to say, always be careful, and when you've got a gun, always be more careful. Not that I ever had a gun, or wanted a gun. What awful things. I can't think why men have to have them and you're just boys. Boys. There's quite enough shooting in the world without English boys doing it as well. And you're quite old enough to know better, sixteen I should think. You're not a boy, you're a young man. There, that should be all right. I think. No, you should always be careful. Look before you leap—'

'Aim before you fire,' said Mike, coldly. He joined Rodney in the study. Each of them was handed a cider and three pound notes.

'I must admit you've earned it,' said the Colonel. 'That was a good battle. A good game. Your friend will be all right. I'll see to him. Doctor's on his way.'

Rodney, folding his money, said:

'I don't think I'd like to do it for a living.'

'Real little gladiators. All good fun anyway. All good friends, all taken in good part.'

'Something new,' said Rodney, sniffing his drink. 'Try anything once.'

He was still fairly drunk.

'It makes you feel good, doesn't it?' asked the Colonel. 'Makes you feel good? I always used to feel good after stalking, I know. More than just ... sport. Bit of a test. Yes. A test. But this other boy's people, d'you know them?'

'People?' asked Mike, staring at the carpet. The carpet seemed to be very deep.

'Parents. His parents. D'you know them? What are they?'

'Hasn't got any, really,' said Rodney. 'Lives on his own. Doesn't work either. Well, not usually. Will he be all right?'

'Don't worry about him. He can stay here for the time being. Don't think he should be moved. Unless the doctor says so. But there is something else. You won't chat about this little game to all and sundry, will you?'

'Well, Mike'll have to explain to his mum how he got scalped.'

'Well, a bit of a scrap, you could say, or you fell down some stairs. Anyway, you won't tell anyone else, parents, friends? Might look bad, to some people you know. You know I'm, I'm, you know what I am ... well, you know as well as I do that I'm MP for Belston. And people might misunderstand the game, ha?'

'Suppose it might look a bit silly,' said Rodney.

'That's just it. Exactly. People wouldn't see that it was just, well, what it was – a game. Don't understand you know. People are fussy these days. Mollycoddlers.'

Rodney laughed at the word. The Colonel began to laugh with him, then stopped himself. He looked from Rodney, so safe and decent, to the dangerously silent Mike. Mike had a lean face. His teeth were bad. His collar was frayed. His mother was poor. His father was dead. The Colonel was guessing correctly. He looked away from Mike.

'Do you both feel like playing this game again, some time? You did it very well indeed. Same prizes?'

The Colonel put his head on one side in a parody of charm. Rodney shook his head suddenly, not to refuse for any logical reason, but because the shock of the shootings had finally reached him.

'What about it then, ha, do you? Bit of fun, no harm done. Bit of fun. Make a man of you.'

'I don't think so,' said Rodney.

'It's fine practice. You boys get something from it, you know. You may not realize it now, but later in life – why, then you'll know what I mean. What are the words? Not real experience, you'll only find that in a real war. But perhaps a scent of glory, a sniff, a whiff of greatness. No medals, ha! But a touch of, a hint of courage. Courage. And that's real. That's really all that's real. Come on boys, we'll try it again, shall we? Next weekend?'

Mike stood up. He took three steps to the desk, sniffed deeply, drawing the snot down into his mouth and then spat into the Colonel's right eye. It was a second before the Colonel put up his hand to wipe away the stinging mess.

'That's all, yes, that's all,' said Mike. 'And you'd better get Jack to hospital. And I'm making no promises not to talk.'

The Colonel gulped his whisky. Between heavy, brief laughs he said: 'I wonder if you know any other boys who enjoy shooting, who might care to earn some money? You know, the game. Do you?'

Rodney shook his head.

Mike said: 'Just show us where you've put Jack. Don't talk to us any more. We've had you. I got no spit left. Where's Jack?'

Upstairs in the Blue Room, Jack lay naked under blankets. His hand still shielded his wounded eye. He was gasping. As she stroked his shoulders with one clever hand, Lorna was saying:

'It's all right. You're a stupid boy, but you'll be all right.'

Mike and Rodney came in.

'Your friends are here,' Lorna said. 'But you'd better tell them to go. The doctor's coming. He said on the phone you mustn't talk.'

Out of his pain, Jack whispered: 'Piss off. Piss off now. Just want that doctor.'

Mike said: 'OK.'

As Mike and Rodney cycled home, Rodney said nothing. Mike swore continuously.

The Colonel marched into the kitchen and confronted his wife.

'Food,' he shouted, then swiped her aside and swung open the cupboard, pulling out the brandy bottle. He poured and swallowed.

'I'm sorry, I'm sorry, it's not ready yet,' she cried, moving deftly to the far side of the table. He picked a fresh brown loaf from the table, tore off a lump and began to consume it. More brandy. He thumped the loaf on the enamel-topped table, chipped like all enamel-topped tables. Stained stainless steel knives rattled in the drawer.

'By God,' he shouted. 'By God, Jane, I'm a bad husband, aren't I?'

'I'm sorry about the lunch.'

'I'm not hungry. I'm a bad husband.'

Suddenly he saw that bloody plastic bowl again. He was too angry to speak. He took another drink. Jane trembled. Her tears began. The Colonel was pulling off his jacket. Her voice became unnaturally loud as she cried:

'I'm going to Bath. I'm going to live at Dorothy's. I'm going to Bath.'

'You can go to Bath or go to Hell, but first I'm going to give you what I like to give you.'

Then he began to tickle her. He forced her over the kitchen table and tickled her badly, painfully, at length. It was a punishment he favoured. Then he let her go, now crying of course and bruised of course, and he smiled and sat and concentrated on his brandy.

An hour later Jack had been taken by Dr Clewes to the cottage hospital. A taxi waited for Jane outside the Hall. It contained three suitcases. Jane returned to the kitchen. The Colonel still sat there.

'I'm going to Bath, to Dorothy's.'

He made no sign to her.

'I need a little money.'

No longer dangerous, he fumbled for his full wallet.

'You'll have to leave Parliament,' she said. 'It's no good. You need a doctor.'

'I don't care to leave the Commons,' he said. 'They need me there, all my friends are there. It's a middling good club.'

'You'll have to leave all that,' she said gently. 'I'm sorry, but you can't go on. I'm going to tell them about that poor boy. He's going to lose an eye.'

Tell them? It didn't matter who she meant by them. Even if

she only told Dorothy, it would be the end of his life outside the Hall. It would come to court. The end. The Colonel, his brain hurting, pushed a pound note into her hand. Her eyes were empty. Another pound note, then two five-pound notes. She wasn't looking at him. Her eyes were focused upon Bath.

'No, Jane. You couldn't.'

His voice sounded weak.

'I must. Of course I must.'

She could, and, knowing her, she would. During all her years of humiliation, she must have been waiting for this cold revenge. He passed her more five-pound notes until his wallet was empty. She took it all, but not as a bribe. There was nothing in her eyes. She walked out.

The Colonel lapped another brandy as he read the list of contents on a sauce bottle, then all four sides of a cereal packet, then a recipe for eggless cake printed on wartime paper. His mind became blanker and blanker until all but a few lumps of thought were dissolved. He went to his study and dialled a number.

'Devon here.'

'Hello, James. Good to hear your voice.'

The Colonel sounded as natural as he could.

'Ah, Colonel, good afternoon. Wonderful day.'

'Good. I just rang to say—'

Pause. A long pause.

'Hello, Colonel. You're still there?'

'Yes, well. Just wanted to say—'

'Yes?'

'Good luck. Something's come up. Wanted to wish you good luck with my – with the constituency. It's a good constituency. Yes. And you'll make a good Member. But I shan't be able to. Yes. Goodbye.'

He hung up for ten seconds, then took the phone off the hook.

James Devon didn't let his bewilderment last long. For some obscure drunken reason, his accession had been promised by the incumbent Member. If he knew why, he would be bound, as a gentleman, to try to dissuade the Colonel from resigning. The dear old drunk. Devon had already been chosen to succeed him at the next General Election, but this sounded like a surprise by-election, a key by-election it would be called, himself defending the 4,578 Tory majority on the platform, in the spotlight, in the National Press and on his home ground, television. In his mind he began to compose a devastatingly casual appeal to the electorate. Perhaps he should be interviewed by some reasonably unsympathetic young man:

'Mr Devon, you're extremely well-known to viewers as a TV personality, the mainstay of quizzes and anchor man of the Great Murders series. But how does this qualify you to represent the ordinary people of Belston?'

'Well, Bob, that's all very flattering.' Puff on pipe, expel smoke in cloud directed between interviewer Bob and camera one. 'But in fact I don't spend much of my time in these places – TV studios. You'll usually find me tramping round a field in my big rubber boots – you know, I've got a small farm just outside Belston. Or, often as not, you'll find me in the fair city of Belston itself, talking to my many good town friends over a tankard of ale.'

'And what do you find to talk to them about?'

A querulous note in the imaginary Bob's voice sounded as if he doubted the existence of those many good friends.

'Well, Bob, I'm not a great one for talk myself, but I like to listen to people's sorrows and their joys as well. And their troubles, great and small. Sometimes I'm lucky enough to be able to help.'

A saddened smile.

'Young marrieds trying to buy their first home. The old people. The sick. Mothers with growing children. Ah, but mostly we mull over what's happening in the big world and what's happening in our own small world. The price of bacon *and* the price of freedom. The fortunes of Belston Rovers – that's the team for me, Bob – and the fortunes of Mr Castro. You know, Bob, you can get a far sight better political education in a friendly inn than you'll get at most of those big colleges.'

Bob (London School of Economics): 'And what do you find the people of Belston really want?'

'Well, Bob, as you know, I'm a Belstonian myself, and I can say that we're not the greediest people in the world. But we do like to work things out for ourselves. We like to run our own businesses and our own lives. And we're not too happy, I can tell you, when people from outside, who don't know Belston, make a lot of rules for Belston folk. We're just a little bit – independent. Pig-headed, if you like, Bob. Now I'd say that a lot of these socialists and their friends are decent, well-meaning people, but God helps those who ...'

James Devon switched on his tape-recorder and started all over again. The effete voice which he adopted for the interviewer Bob contrasted with his own deeper, tweedy, sincere tones.

Carrying his loaded shot-gun and talking to it as he walked down the worn stone steps, Colonel Munche entered the Hall's vast cellar and switched on its stark lights. There were many full and empty bottles, a few dirty glasses, a leather-padded couch and three trunks full of pornographic books and magazines which the Colonel had collected during his career in many lands or bought while he was drunk in London. Privately he called this cobweb-cornered stone room his pornocellar. Empty-headed as a baby, the Colonel laid himself gently on the couch and blew out his brains. The pain stopped almost as soon as it began.

'I shall return to Bath the day after the funeral,' said Mrs Munche as her fingers rapidly smoothed the tissue paper between the dresses in her trunk. The Reverend Realeigh was perturbed.

'So soon, Mrs Munche? Perhaps a little holiday would be the best thing. I always find that a holiday—'

He stopped to avoid a truism. Mrs Munche looked quite strong, stronger than usual. She folded a corset, then looked him in the eyes.

'It is not a holiday, Vicar, it's for good. I shall stay with my friend Dorothy as a paying guest.'

'But ... the Hall?'

'The Hall belongs to my daughter.'

'But surely she will need your companionship at this time?'

Mrs Munche smiled.

'You don't know Lorna.'

'I, I confirmed her. I still remember. It was her grandmother's confirmation dress, was it not?'

Immediately he said 'was it not?' he regretted the phrase. Too stilted, too like the Vicar in a Home Counties murder play. He had acted in several such plays. The phrase 'I expect you are wondering why I called you all together tonight' passed through his mind. He suspected ill-will between the mother and daughter in this house. Who was responsible? Was there any connection between their apparent distaste for each other and the apparent suicide of the Colonel? Perhaps he should do something to reconcile the two women. How could he, when the mother was so determined to leave?

Mrs Munche was indeed unshakable in her decision to leave the scene of her private crime. She had threatened the Colonel with public exposure; in fact, she had promised him disgrace. So he had killed himself. The only wonder was, he hadn't killed her. She was not sure who to be grateful to for that.

'I'm afraid I can't remember the dress. But Lorna is perfectly capable of looking after herself, and the Hall. She has a remarkable memory. And most capable. The—'

She had been going to say 'The Colonel used to say', but she was afraid to talk about him. She might give something away, the tell-tale heart, the twitching of an eye. She would never even be able to tell Dorothy what she had done.

'Mrs Munche, are you quite sure you're doing the right thing?'

'I have done it,' she said. 'Lorna is very rich now.'

As she slammed the trunk and dragged another one from under the bed, the Vicar winced.

'You will be at the funeral, of course.'

'Of course. And the next day I shall travel to Bath. On the train. I think I shall travel first class. The waiters are exceptionally clean and they even say thank you to each other. So, if you will excuse me, Vicar . . .'

He took a large breath. The room smelled pleasantly of lavender. He decided against commenting on this minor delight. To mention the subject of odour when there was a corpse in the house would be tactless.

'Mrs Munche, I came here because I very much wanted to offer you comfort.'

She smiled vaguely.

'Comfort?'

It was going to be an effort, it was probably hardly worth it, she didn't want succour, but it had to be offered just in case. He would rather have been an actor than a parson, but he was aware that his movements were not good enough.

'God knows all,' he said. 'And God is love. I know that sounds simple, even a little childish perhaps; I couldn't say that sort of thing to the youth down at the club. With them perhaps I would draw a parable from the lyrics of a pop record, which might be equally childish, equally simple, but nevertheless ... Mrs Munche – however deep your mourning, however dark your grief, however bleak the shock to your heart – God knows. He knows.'

Supposing He did know, what was He doing about it? The Revd Realeigh just didn't know.

Mrs Munche had been looking out of the window towards the fake heathen temple. He could not see if she looked touched or comforted or not.

'Comfort?' she said. 'I'm very comfortable, thank you.'

The Vicar winced again, consciously overcame a major inhibition which dated from his days and nights in boarding school, and touched her lightly on the shoulder, or rather touched the surface of the dress which covered her shoulder.

'You're a very brave lady, Mrs Munche, if I may say so.'

What a namby-pamby phrase, he told himself. 'If I may say so' – nervous, unmanly, undermining the straight-from-the shoulder certainty of his 'God knows' speech. For a moment he wondered if Mrs Munche had, by some incredible omission, not been informed of her husband's death. An awful old joke passed through his mind. ('Good morning Widow Munche.' 'My name's Munche, but I'm no widow.' 'You wait till you see what they're bringing up from the cellar.') The Vicar kicked himself internally, then tiptoed from the room to find Lorna. Unfortunately he didn't know where she was, so he moved from door to door, knocking discreetly on each. There was no answer upstairs, so he went down the wide front stairway and began again. Door after door.

Lorna was in her late father's study, sitting at the desk, working her way through a tumbler full of red Martini. Her eyeballs were clustered with red veins caused by sleeplessness, smoking and drinking. She had not cried. Her mind was concentrated. She was calm now.

'Vicar. Mr Realeigh. You'll have a drink?'

Policemen in plays always said, 'I'm afraid we're not allowed to drink while we're on duty ma'am.' But the Vicar liked sherry, so he had one. He trusted himself with sherry, even with the enormous helping poured by Lorna. At forty-seven years old, he could hold his liquor – a worldly phrase that – without any physical qualms. He sat on the edge of the sofa, held his tumbler between the soft palms of his hands, and stared into it. After a suitable period of silence, he looked up.

'My dear Lorna, what can I do to help you?'

Lorna started beating one foot, first the toe, then the flat heel, on the floor, reciting in time to the beat:

'Help, help, that's all right. That's all right. You can't raise him from the dead, can you? You can't do that old trick? You haven't got a little black bag with a Lazarus Conjuring Set in it, have you?'

The Vicar gave a forgiving smile and shook his head.

'That's all right then, just asking, that's all right.'

She seemed ill. It must have been a shock to her psyche. The Vicar had been taught that suicide was a cowardly sin, but that was one of the pieces of ecclesiastical knowledge which he never passed on. It never seemed appropriate. To express it in a more sturdy way, it never came in handy. Besides, he had considered suicide himself and had found himself too cowardly to do it.

'What can I do?' he asked.

'You can ask me again.'

'Ask you what?'

'The Catechism. Ask me the Catechism.'

He could see she was drunk, somewhat drunk, understandably so, and probably, through a combination of grief and alcohol, near to hysteria. However, it might be possible, by co-operating with her whims, to soothe the girl. And so he began:

'What is your Name?'

'Lorna.'

'Who gave you this Name?'

'My father. My mother agreed. I think I was called after some island where he fought or was stationed or something. But I don't know. I was never curious about it before. I knew I was Lorna, and that's all I wanted the name to mean.'

'What did your Godfathers and Godmothers do then for you?'

'They did promise and vow three things in my name. But you know how it is. I couldn't renounce the devil and all his works because most of the time I didn't believe in the devil, and when I did – I was about eleven at the time – I was so scared of him that I couldn't renounce him. The pomps and vanities – I never saw much pomp except the Coronation and I liked that, wishing it could be me. And I use make-up when I go into town, so I suppose I'm vain and all that. Secondly, that I should believe all the Articles. Well, you told me at the time that so long as I tried, it would be all right. That didn't work, I couldn't believe in every one of them. Bet you can't either. And keeping God's will and his Commandments, I suppose that's a matter of opinion, but I've been pretty random about keeping them, pretty random I'd say.'

'You don't want to go on talking like this, surely Lorna? I can be no party to blasphemy.'

But it was Lorna's party. She filled his glass.

'What party? What blasphemy? This is going to be the truth. You don't run a confessional, but please let me talk. It does me so much good. There's nobody else I can tell.'

The Revd Realeigh had read enough reviews of books about psychology to understand her demand. Let her talk. Lance the boil, let the poison flow. That didn't sound very healthy. Good sherry. He asked, returning to the routine:

'Dost thou not think that thou art bound to believe, and to do, as they have promised for thee?'

'Well, one of my godparents was an atheist anyway, even if he was a knight. But I understand you in a sort of distant way. Yes, I am bound. I don't know about the belief part of it. But I am bound, I know that, I'm bound. I can't choose. I'm bound.'

'Rehearse the Articles of thy Belief.'

'I believe in my father, who became a Colonel. And in Lorna Munche, his only daughter, who was conceived by my father, the dead Colonel, born of the Virgin bride my mother. Suffered little, was educated, fed and deflowered. Lorna, Lorna who found her father's body in the cellar. She knew what to do. She stood up. She stands up and holds her dead father's dead hand. From thence she shall come to judge.

'And I believe in my father; in his estate, in the rule of those who are fit to rule, in my own decisions, in my triumph, my permanent triumph. Amen.'

'What dost thou chiefly learn in these Articles of Belief?'

'First, I learn to believe in my father, who hath made me and all my world.

'Secondly, in myself. I know what to do.

'Thirdly, in my dead father, who justifies me and talks with me, and in all those who fight on my father's side.'

'You said, that your Godfathers and Godmothers did promise for you, that you should keep God's Commandments. Tell me how many there be?'

'Ten.'

'Which be they?'

'The same which my father taught me, saying, "I'm your father, we were poor once, but now we're rich.

'"One. Show some respect for your father.

'"Two. Whoever you marry, I'm your father and I come first. Remember that. I need you, but if you let me down, well, you know I'm not a hard man, I'm really a very weak man, Lorna, but if you let me down, I won't hesitate to cut you off. Cut you off. But I know you won't let me down.

'"Three. Just because you're called Munche – and it's an honourable, respected name – don't bank on it. That name's a privilege and a responsibility. It carries rights but it also carries duties. Remember that.

'"Four. Remember my birthday. If there's one thing I could never forgive you, Lorna, it's forgetting my birthday. Your mother once forgot my birthday.

'"Five. Honour thy father and thy mother for that matter.

Remember you'll have to run the estate some day.

'"Six. There's killing and killing. In wartime your duty may include killing. Do your duty and don't brood on it.

'"Seven. Don't mess around with boys. They won't respect you. Keep yourself clean for the man you marry. Otherwise he won't value you. Your mother has always been faithful to me. She saved herself for marriage.

'"Eight. Don't steal. You don't have to. Just run the estate properly. Don't pay the staff too much; they'll ask for more than you can afford, so pay them as little as they'll take. Get my accountant to fix your taxes. Invest in overseas countries which have low wages but stable governments. But don't steal.

'"Nine. Don't let down the side. Of course, you're free to criticize your parents or the Army or Britain or religion or the Party – but don't do it in public.

'"Ten. If you want something, go straight for it. Take it. Within reason, of course."'

Lorna took a bottle and splashed gin into her quarter-full Martini tumbler.

'You're not offending me,' said the Vicar.

Lorna smiled and moved to the sofa, balancing her very full glass with both hands. She continued to smile.

'It does help, you know,' she said.

She pretended to sob, two sobs each lasting half a second at most. Then she put her hand on the black cloth of his shoulder and for the next five minutes, as she talked, manoeuvred it slowly round the back of his neck until it clasped his far shoulder.

'Please, please help me. Ask me all the questions.'

The Vicar sighed and sipped. His stomach was hot with its overdose of sherry.

'What dost thou chiefly learn by these Commandments?'

'I learn two things: my duty towards my father, and my duty towards my class.'

That was almost exactly the official prayer-book phraseology.

'What is thy duty towards thy father, I mean, I'm sorry, what is thy duty towards thy God?'

'My duty towards my dead father is to believe in him, to fear him, and to love him with all my heart, with all my mind, with all my soul; and with all my strength to worship him, to give him thanks, to put my whole trust in him, to call upon him, to honour his rank and his advice, and to serve him truly all the days of my life.'

'What is thy duty towards thy Neighbour?'

'My duty towards my class is to love it as myself and not to betray it. To love, honour and succour my dead father and my mother as well; to honour and obey the Queen and her Government; to submit myself to all priests, teachers and tutors; to respect the Law; to avoid giving offence; to keep my word; to keep my temper; to keep my hands from showing disrespect for property, and my tongue from gossip about my betters; to keep my hole for my husband; not to steal, but to gain what I can and to do my duty in that state of life unto which it shall please my dead father to call me.'

'My good Child, know this, that thou art not able to do these things of thyself, nor to walk in the Commandments of God, and to serve him, without his special grace; which thou must learn and at all times call for by diligent prayer. Let me hear, therefore, if thou canst recite, I mean, say the Lord's Prayer.'

They both drank.

'My father, wherever you are – I love you. I'll look after the estate. I'll do what you wanted me to do. Let my income increase. I'm sorry I never let you, I know you're sorry you tried but you needn't have been—'

'– You don't know what you're saying—'

'No,' she said. 'I don't know what I'm saying.'

Again she appeared to sob. Her arm tightened around his neck. Her face, hidden against his dark lapel, smiled as he coughed and then breathed more heavily. She shifted her soft weight against him. After a silent minute, she jumped up, switched on a light, drew the curtains and locked the door. He was afraid now, but her return hounded out his fear. As she pulled off her sweater he was struggling with his unwieldy collar. Soon her hands were marching all over his inept, pale body. She beleaguered him, captured him and destroyed him. As they dressed again, before she sent him, all pink, back to his wife, he said:

'Lorna, what can I do?'

'Nothing. After the funeral you had better live your life until you die.'

'What will you do?'

'I know who killed my father. He killed himself – well, I know that. Anybody knows that. But I know why. He got these three boys, they were poachers, shooting his rabbits, he got these three boys to play a game. And one of them wounded one of the others, in the eye, with an air-gun. In the game. Father paid them, they should have been happy enough, he did pay them. But mother told me that the boys said they'd tell people about father's game. And it wouldn't have sounded good, would it? Father would have had to give up his seat in the Commons. He couldn't face that, you know he couldn't. He'd have had to leave the Hall. He couldn't do that. So he killed himself. So I know what to do now. I'm going to kill those boys.'

'Lorna, you can't do that.'

'I'm not going to shoot them or strangle them or poison them. But I'll destroy them. One by one. That's legal. That's easy. I'll just destroy them. They will end up as destroyed people. You see? You will see. I won't even leave their bones.'

She lifted her eyes to the ceiling and let him go. He scrambled into the rest of his clothes. But as he climbed into his Mini, Lorna mounted Masterman. For a quarter of a mile she galloped beside the car, shouting obscenities at him.

Two days later, after the inquest, the Vicar was back, weakly querying Lorna's unorthodox ideas for the funeral.

'My mother has nothing to do with the burial now. My mother's not present. She flew. Fled. She's immersing herself in Bath, embalming herself, whatever you like.'

'My dear Lorna, that may well be. Your poor mother wants to build a new life for herself, to renew herself even, to rip herself away from the Hall and all its memories. But she still has feelings. She is, after all, a widow—'

'– She's a happy old widow at that, sailing up and down the streets admiring the hats and the stonework, feeling herself young again among all those cronies. She's a technical widow, that's all. If you saw her in a restaurant and called out:

"Widow! Hey, widow!" she'd be the last to turn round. Look at this letter, look at the way she writes, she always used black ink before, now it's blue on blue paper. That's how she feels. Look at the ribbony loops of her handwriting. No jaggedness any more.'

The Vicar read the letter.

Dear Lorna,

Here I am in Bath! At last! Although I travelled First, the man opposite me, although his suit was very expensive, had very large shoes which must have been worn and *not cleaned* for at least two weeks! I would have taken him for a schoolmaster – if he had been travelling Third – but he said that he was working for a newspaper! I was very careful what I said after that! There was a kind of roughness in his voice which should have warned me. He talked *quite* pleasantly about the better people he had met, but ate hardly *anything* during lunch (well, British Railways!) although he did drink *four* bottles of beer. After lunch he became rather churlish about his employers (I did not reveal our financial interest in the *Gazette*, of course), and so I retreated into the *Illustrated London News*, which always makes me feel young again. Soon we arrived in Bath Spa station, and there was Dorothy, just the same as ever! She had requisitioned a taxi to *sweep* us up the hill to her flat. Tea was all ready for us (prepared by Mouse, her maid). We sat up until nearly midnight, talking and scheming. Don't faint dear, but we might start a shop! Just for fun, of course, and we would only sell things we really liked ourselves, really beautiful things. Dorothy has marvellously good taste.

Oh dear, business. You know, darling, I could not *face* staying at the Hall for the funeral and I think your idea for a quiet interment on the estate is *just right*. (I have not discussed this with Dorothy, as I think she might find the idea a little *jarring*.) I can hardly bring myself to think about it, but you are so strong, perhaps you can, as you say, manage without your useless little mother for the next few months. Are you sure? Of course, I give permission for anything you think best. The Hall will be all yours when the Will is made absolute, plus half the Colonel's shares. The rest will be in trust with me. I almost forgot to send you money. I have made out a cheque for two thousand pounds for you to be jogging along with. If you would like, do come and see us in Bath. We could arrange for you to stay in a very nice private hotel nearby. At *Christmastime* anyway!

Your loving MUMMY

'Now ring my lawyer,' said Lorna. 'He was at the inquest. He says everything's all right.'

She dialled, was clicked through to the solicitor, and introduced him, over the cross-country, whining telegraph wires, to the Vicar, who said:

'Frankly, this is an entirely new situation for me. You're quite sure that it's in order? And the memorial tablet? I see ...'

Lorna was already back at the desk. As she wrote two funeral invitations, the Vicar put the phone quietly down. He looked at Lorna's back, committed adultery in his heart, and waited.

To Rodney it seemed, overwhelmingly, the decent thing to do. As he walked down the Grammar School corridor, greeting friends and masters with an automatic, spread, upraised hand or a respectfully smiling nod, he tried to convince Mike that they should go. Mike trailed his fingers along the red tiles lining the corridor and could think of nothing to say in return.

Mike's feelings about the Colonel were as odd as his feelings about the rest of the world. The Colonel was a cartoon figure who had died a cartoon death. But then Rodney was something of a cartoon, and Mike had a fondness for Rodney. And Jack, before he lost his eye, seemed intent on turning himself into a cartoon character, and Mike liked Jack a lot. And as Mike thought about himself, he saw himself as a cartoon character in a cartoon world in which the nations behaved like comedy cats and mice – well surely their exploits could not involve real pain, they were too cruel, it must be a cartoon.

As Rodney and Mike pushed, side by side, out on to the school steps to stare down the driveway, Mike saw, on the left-hand side of the drive, a man raking the brown, soggy leaves into piles. At the far end of the drive, fourth-formers were shoving each other into the neat pyramids of leaves, shampooing each other with clumps of the thin, rotting litter from the trees. Rodney approved the raker and disapproved of the boys. Mike reckoned the raker should be given something more satisfying to do and decided that the best way to treat dead leaves would be to let them merge and sink into the ground in their own time to nourish the roots of the trees.

'Don't you feel it's our responsibility to go to the funeral?' Rodney asked.

Mike shrugged, hitched his pile of books higher under his arm.

'There'll probably be hundreds of people there,' Rodney said. 'You wouldn't have to talk to anyone.'

'I didn't know him.'

'We met him.'

'All right, but we're not related. We weren't mates, were we? Me and the Colonel, Christ – we were like *that*.'

Mike raised two fingers in an up-you sign.

'What about that girl, his daughter? She wants us to come, otherwise she wouldn't have written.'

'That girl, well, she's weird. I don't know why she asked us, but it's peculiar. Isn't it?'

'She – maybe she liked us. Maybe she doesn't know many people.'

'That why you want to go? Think she fancies you? Or is she after me? Reckon we'll both get our ends away after the dust-to-dust bit?'

'You're scared to go.'

'I only went to one funeral in my life and that was my dad. It was terrible. I didn't believe a word they said. All that big talk about God. As if God ever did anything for my dad.'

'You are scared.'

'Maybe. I don't like funerals. I didn't like the Colonel.'

'It'd be interesting.'

'Interesting? What, you want to see how rich people get buried? What's in it for you? Interesting? Shall we take cameras? You want to know what they eat afterwards? How they get drunk? Want to see if they cry like real people? Christ, if you're interested you'd better go, if you're that interested. Get it out of your system. Where are you going for your holidays? Hiroshima. Very interesting place, Hiroshima—'

'Lay off, that's got nothing—'

'Come on Rod, we've got half an hour before the end of visiting time. Come and see Jack – he's lost an eye. Should be interesting.'

Rodney hit him in the ribs, pulling his punch at the last moment. They ran for their bikes in a parody of Battle of

Britain pilots scrambling for their Spitfires, took off and zoomed to the hospital. The pretty, harsh-voiced nurse told them they could only see Jack for ten minutes.

'He's still rather shocked.'

Jack was propped up, his dead eye covered with gauze. He didn't say anything at first, but reached for the tea-mug on his locker, swivelled it slowly to his lips, drank twice and said:

'What's the news?'

Mike began to tell him about the thefts, or suspected thefts, or rumoured suspected thefts from the changing-rooms, but Jack, without smiling, cut him off.

'What about the funeral? Are you going?'

'I don't see why we should. Look what the Colonel did for us,' said Mike quickly, pointing to Jack's bandage. But Jack angrily covered the bandage with his hand and said:

'That's nothing to do with it. Are you going?'

Rodney said: 'We should, really, it wouldn't hurt us. And they obviously want us to go. She wants us to go.'

'Oh yes,' said Jack. 'She wants you to go all right. You better go, I think, you ought to go to that funeral thing.'

He was talking very quietly, very flatly, with authority. Mike leaned forward from the heavy chair, rested his elbows on the rail at the bottom of the bed and asked:

'Why?'

'Because. Because. Because, I saw that girl, Lorna. The horse girl. That girl was here when I came out of the gas. All right. Her dad's dead. All right. Killed himself. All right? But when she came down here to see me, she sat there, in that chair where you are, just sat there, held the basin when I was sick, didn't say anything, didn't look disgusted, helped me to clean my mouth out. I tried to tell her she could go home, she ought to, but it just came out of my mouth like a moan. She took hold of my hand. Don't grin. She took hold of my hand. It was, it was – I knew she would have let go if I wanted her to, or held my hand harder if I wanted her to. She sat there a long time. She stayed hours. All right. She wants you at the funeral. All right, so I want you at it too.'

From far away they could see her standing completely still between the pillars of the Hall; legs apart, gloved hands on hips, black dress billowing around her calves, the black spotted veil of her hat pushed back from her face. Standing still, but the strength of the wind changed the shape of the blackness of her costume every second. They lowered their bicycles to the gravel and walked up the steps to her, Rodney's hands clasping each other, Mike's hands scratching at the dust-clogged corners of his suit's trouser-pockets.

Her voice was low today: a clarinet.

'Thank you for coming. Will you meet the others?'

She took them to the study. The desk was covered by a sheet. She introduced them to the Revd Realeigh and a Mr Beevers.

She gave them each a normal-sized sherry and left them forming a black-suited, uneasy square. Rodney asked the Vicar:

'Are there many, um, many more mourners to come?'

The Vicar looked away, nodding his head at the window, more nervous than he had been at his first funeral. Who put the fun in funeral? he thought. Then he returned to thinking about the shape of Lorna's face.

'I believe this is, er, all. Although the grave-diggers will of course be present. A very quiet ceremony. Yes.'

Immediately he had spoken, he tried to remember what he had just said. Impossible. Lorna's face.

'We're the only ones, then?' asked Rodney.

'Um, yes. I believe so. You see ... you understand ... the circumstances?'

Mike said: 'Yes,' firmly.

Mr Beevers took a step forward, paused for a second, then in a perfectly controlled torrent of professional whispering, explained his function:

'Of course, the law concerning funeral arrangements allows the utmost latitude, for it has to take into consideration the personal feelings and beliefs of many, many different and contrasted individuals and sects, and of course there is nothing, nothing at all extra-legal about the ceremony today, but, since the Colonel was such a prominent figure and since interment in a private house is, to say the least, unusual, Miss Munche thought it might be as well if her legal representative were present. To allay any misgivings, that is. I am Miss Munche's solicitor.'

Mike said: 'But he's not being buried inside the house, is he?'

'Oh yes,' said Mr Beevers. 'Definitely yes, and he might have been buried almost anywhere. But, well it's not as if he were going to be interred in this room, for instance. The interment will be in the cellar, and a cellar, one might say, is the secular equivalent of a vault or crypt. Not so, Padre?'

In the Vicar's mind, Lorna's face shuddered and dissolved.

'Quite so. Rather like a crypt interment. Yes.'

Lorna came into the room, moving into the group and out again saying:

'We are ready.'

They paraded down the stairs to the cellar; first Lorna, stepping carefully, then the Vicar, then Mike who turned for a second to grimace at Rodney, and after Rodney, Mr Beevers, who had produced a small red notebook. The cellar was enormous. At its far end was a heavy tower of trunks, crates, shapes, shadows reaching up to the stone ceiling. At the centre of the cellar two huge paving stones had been levered aside. There was a stack of very pale earth, a new white flagstone and two workmen carrying spades. The mourners stood about the pit and looked down, seeing, in the dusk of the grave, a bulging Union Jack. Lorna handed the Vicar a page of typescript. He looked at her appealingly, but she looked away and stared down at her father. The Revd Realeigh began to read aloud, slowly and rhythmically, the words which she had written and had forced him to rehearse:

'There he lies, where we have put him, wrapped in the flag which he served and loved. It has been announced that he took his own life. He would laugh at that. He saw men who took their own lives in the trenches of France, but he was strong. He was stronger than any of us. He died under attack. He died in action.

'He was a regular soldier. He laughed when he heard fat, slumbering civilians talk about peace glibly. Only a soldier knows what the word peace means. It is always wartime. The Colonel knew that, he knew that everything he valued was constantly under attack, and that when even the least of these values was under attack, he himself was under attack. And so he died, died in action.

'We are left standing round his grave, smaller than he was, less courageous, less single-minded, less. Our choice is this – either to continue his work or to abandon it, either to honour him or to dishonour him. That is the choice. And even as we would have been afraid to dishonour him during his lifetime, so now, we should be afraid to dishonour him in death. He died in action.

'God rest his soul.'

The workmen looked at Lorna, who nodded once. Earth began to cover the Union Jack, to fill the pit. The Vicar wept steadily, Mr Beevers had written nothing in his notebook, Rodney's left eye was bothering him. At one end of the filling grave stood Mike, his face taut with anger. He did not understand his own anger, except he felt that a curse had just been laid upon him. At the other end of the grave stood Lorna, her face, entangled in its black net, challenging his anger.

The nurses in the amateur-looking cottage hospital kept telling Jack that he looked like a pirate with that patch, but he liked them. Though they wore starched white armour over their busts, when they stood in profile you could see behind their breastplates the fine blue and white stripes following lineaments of infinite comfort. If you're mending well, hospitals carry a high sex-charge.

On Jack's third day alone in a ward designed for five people, he lowered himself into a chair stamped with the initials of the Hospital Board and stared one-eyed into an empty mirror – no, of course, it was a window. A very conscientious window, letting in a great deal of light, just doing its job, more than its job would be worth to let in darkness, you bet. Jack sat, crowned with cigarette smoke, on his canvas throne, clicking his toes with pleasure to the tune in his head, only slightly irritated to discover that the melody was 'Mary, Mary, Quite Contrary'.

There was a rubber hum, footsteps, and in came a wheelchair carrying company. The new patient was persuaded into bed. A fey, long-legged boy whose hair had been cropped by an idiot barber. His feet were bandaged. He looked like a silly, red-lipped gnome.

Jack pushed himself to his feet and shuffled in his ratepayers' slippers back to bed. After three days alone, except for the nurses with their functional conversation and fleeting breasts, he felt like talking.

'Hello. How are you?'

Jack realized he'd forgotten how to speak, except in phrase-book English. The answer came back fast and high-pitched in weirdly jumbled diction.

'I'm all right. I'm all right. Have you had an operation too, eh? With knives? I had one to my feet, to my feet, and I can't walk for a bit. You can walk on your feet. I saw you so you can walk on your feet. My feet are all right, but I can't walk on them. I had an operation to them. Did you have an operation with knives?'

'Sort of. I just hurt my eye, that's all.'

'Hurt your eye? Eye? Eyes are very soft. Did someone hit you very hard, eh? Was it someone very big who hit your eye with something hard?'

'No. I fell off a toboggan sliding down a pyramid. Could've happened to anyone. In fact it was supposed to happen to Sir Alec Douglas-Home, but it was his day off ...'

The boy didn't laugh. But he smiled a long smile.

Jack: 'What's your name?'

'Charles. I was named after someone called Charles, I think, but I'm not sure which Charles. There have been many famous Charleses. Kings, too. Charles the First. They cut off his head with an axe. Charles the Second. Prince Charles who will be Charles the Third and Charles Dickens and many others. I'm Charles, too.'

'My name's Jack. How long have you—'

'Hey, Jack. Do you know about electric fences, eh?'

'About what?'

'Electric fences, because, have you ever seen electric fences? You know, wire they put round fields, in the country, only they're electric. Have you seen them? I've heard about them but I don't think I've seen them. There are such things as electric fences, aren't there? I mean, it's not a lie about electric fences in the country?'

'Yes, I mean, no it's not a lie. There are electric fences.'

'Have you seen electric fences?'

'Think so. Yes, I have.'

'Where, where did you see them, eh?'

'Only a few miles from here, I think.'

The interrogation became merciless. Though his brain was vague and hot and his eye hurt, Jack was pushed into describing, drawing and explaining as best he could, the electric fence which he thought he remembered seeing a few miles away. The only thing he could remember for sure was that Mike knew someone who once pissed on an electric fence and got a cock shock, but he didn't want to tell that story to this odd child. For two hours their lopsided conversation moved from the nature of electric shocks to the name of the inventor of the electric fence ('Maybe he was called Mr Fence,' was Jack's best guess), to the effect of the fence on cattle and whether it could be true that they observed the boundary the fence set even after the fence had been taken away. They discussed, with mutual ignorance, the cost of an electric fence, insulation methods, the nature of the appropriate shock machine or dynamo or electric pump which powered it, and eventually they circled back to the raw subject of electric shocks. Finally Jack was desperate to escape from the conversation. The boy had been probing him intolerably, stupidly, indecently, pushing aside his own defensive questions and diversionary attempts, his big eyes flickering round the walls as if in search of an electric fence.

'I'm going to read now, Charles. Have you any books?'

'Yes, er, yes, I've got books, a big pile of books. In my locker. Full of books, reading books.'

'Well, we'll both have a bit of a read. Right?'

'Will you read to me? I can't read.'

'I – how old are you, then?'

Jack's automatic, instantly regretted question drifted off into a short silence. The answer came flatly:

'I'm fourteen.'

The boy was very retarded. A spastic? Jack couldn't ask that. He knew even less about spastics than electric fences. He'd seen the sad posters, had bought the little paper flags, magical signs to ward off disease. It was a bad word, spastic, painting in Jack's mind a kind of science-fiction race, plastic people. 'Spastic' scared Jack in the same way that 'leper' had terrified him in scripture lessons. It was a word that couldn't be looked in the eyes. It might turn you to stone. Jack had never said 'spastic' out loud in his life.

He read to the boy slowly, interrupted by questions about electric shocks and wire – subjects wildly unrelated to the balloon-happy world of the Moomins. Jack was beginning to enjoy Moominland when Charles let loose a yell, a high war-whoop:

'Nurse! Nurse!'

She bundled in, the dark Welsh contralto.

'What is it this time?'

Jack was hurt by her impatience with the boy, he couldn't help his need for help. He was a spastic or something, after all, just doing his job – needing help.

'I want to draw. Can I draw, eh? In my drawing-book.'

'Of course you can draw, you don't have to call me just to ask me that, do you Charles?'

'No, nurse. Could you find my pencils? And I've messed the bed.'

She fetched, without comment, a basin, old flannel, clean sheets and a towel. While she cleaned him and his bed, Charles laughed at her, attempting to make jokes about his shit. She just kept going. When Charles and his bed were clean again, she took his crayons and drawing-book from his locker, gave them to him, then left without smiling.

Jack admired her now. Quiet woman of action, good action. He wished she could stay and comfort him with her breasts, or even comfort both of them – one breast each. But she had too much to do. Charles began to draw violently, occasionally tearing the pages of his large, floppy drawing-book, sometimes laughing to himself, whispering tattered phrases, slurred names and jokes which weren't jokes, riddles with the wrong answers. When Jack had to get up to piss, he stopped at Charles's bedside on the way back.

'See your drawings?'

Jack fingered the pages, turning them slowly at first, then more slowly. They were vivid and crude and he would never forget them. Almost every picture showed a fat and owlish face set on top of a burly body. The background held a maze of detail in bright crayoned reds and thick browns. The setting was always the same – a butcher's shop hung with carcases. Conversation became worse and more one-sided. Now the boy wanted to talk about meat.

'How would you like to live in a butcher's shop, eh? What would happen if you sat on an electric fence? I like butcher's shops because of all the dead animals. They put them on hooks, dead animals, in a butcher's shop. They do, you know. Have you ever killed an animal?'

The boy was one of Jack's rabbit victims come to haunt him.

'I'd rather see animals alive. Why don't you draw them alive? You draw very well.'

'But they're better to draw when they're dead. All red, aren't they? I think red is very pretty. Are you pretty?'

The laughter which followed this was repeated after every statement and most questions. Sympathy became more and more difficult. The child couldn't talk without taunting the nurses with his eccentric obscenities, the blood and shit of his talk. At night he rocked himself noisily to sleep. Jack began to wear his radio earphones most of the time, to protect his head. Most of the programmes weren't about meat or electric fences.

Charles's father visited the next evening, staying about half an hour and talking quietly, as if ashamed of talking, as if half dead from lack of sleep, which did not suit his owlish face as it perched on the top of his burly body.

As he left, Lorna arrived. She sat on the bed beside Jack and stroked his cheek until he woke up. Then he had to clear his good eye of gunk before he could see who it was.

At first she was just a blur of white and pink and green and brown. She had chosen a light, low-cut frock for the visit, and she sat close to him. She said nothing, but with her arm lying along the blanket which covered his thigh, she took his hand. She still said nothing, but smiled. Charles was silent, his head clamped in his earphones. After some more minutes, Lorna kissed Jack. Jack suddenly burrowed his face into the pillow as his eye started to cry. He couldn't stop. He was howling for her love, certainly. And he was howling for Charles, because of Charles, Charles on the hook in the butcher's shop. She left him like that. Charles took off his earphones to listen to the crying.

Late that night they brought in an old man. White screens surrounded the bed between Jack and Charles. A quick nurse trundled in the oxygen. Jack could hear the rasping, hard breathing of the old man and the piercing questions from Charles. The nurse whispered to Jack:

'The old boy's got pneumonia.'

The screens were finally folded back, and, for a moment, just before he fell asleep, Jack saw a white face with many lines on it through the expanding and retracting transparent mask.

All next day the old man talked in a waking dream. He insisted that Jack should call him Bill, and offered stories about battles in France and nights in the Yukon, interspersed with dogmatic philosophy. He said he had been in the Gold Rush and Jack eventually believed him, even though Bill had twice referred to it as the God Rush.

'You'd blast the rock, and if you saw the gold staring at you, you'd think you had the whole world. Silly!'

'What did you do when you found it? Did you burst into a saloon and plonk it on the counter like in Westerns?'

'Ah. Find it. I've seen men who've just found gold take it up in their hands like this and eat it, gnaw it like a bone. It makes them mad.'

'Just like that?'

'Yes. I've seen a lot of metals. But gold is different from them all. Platinum, huh. Once I saw Soapy Smith come in and put a handful of gold on the bar while the other fellers were out scratchin' for it.'

Charles interrupted.

'Did you see any dead animals?'

'I don't know, boy. I didn't look for any dead animals.'

'I like dead animals.'

'Well, I like live animals. Most of them. There were some huge beasts out in the Yukon. Huge. Once I saw a caribou so big he took three days to pass the cabin door.'

Jack laughed a lot and the old man was pleased. But Charles only responded with:

'I like dead animals best. In the shop. On hooks. You can see the bones.'

The old man was angered.

'That's plain silly. You're a silly boy.'

'You're silly.'

Their feud was clinched. Arguments bounced to and fro, the old man protesting from his delirium as the boy strummed away on the morbid chords he favoured. One, two, three – dead animals, butcher's hooks, electric fences. One sleepless night Jack sat up in bed, terrified by the thought that he might have been committed to a mental hospital but nobody would tell him. Then his terror turned into a longing to see Lorna. That longing became the fear that she might have left the country. Why shouldn't she? She was rich. She could leave the country any time. Maybe for the Yukon. He saw her leaning mockingly on the stairs of a spittoon-cluttered saloon, her body encircled by one of those red-and-black striped corsets. Now she was being carried by gigantic African bearers between those two famous mountains, the Breasts of Sheba, towards King Solomon's Mines. Now she was dancing indiscreetly with the randy Flamenco dancers of somewhere in Spain, inflamed by sherry, octopus cooked in its own ink and the low cost of living. Or was it squid? Yes, squid. Now her white yacht was easing its way over the fathoms of a blue Caribbean harbour to the muscular chimes of a steel band ...

Next day Mike and Rodney arrived with half a bottle of whisky. This time he didn't mention Lorna to them. Lorna was his friend, not really theirs. And not his, either. Rodney was too guilty to say much. When Mike tried to describe the Colonel's funeral, Jack cut him short.

That night the Welsh nurse tutted at a seventeen-year-old fancying whisky, but nobody objected when he poured a good measure for Bill. The old man was dying, after all. He died after talking in his half-sleep all night, his breathing setting the trudging rhythm of his talk.

He spoke of his dead dog:

'Come here, Bob. Here. Good boy. Uh. He's my dog. He goes. He comes back. I tell him what to do.'

He spoke about the world in general:

'Life is a – damn sight funnier – the longer you live.'

His last words were:

'I meet – all sorts of people – at night. I don't know them –

not – nice people. The Italian – he charged – too much – so I – *cut* – cut – cut him out – yes!'

The day Jack left, Charles was kept busy doing exercises which might help him to walk. He was too exhausted to ask questions about Bill. In the afternoon, as Jack packed his bag, Charles's father came over and thanked him for reading to the boy. He looked even more tired.

Jack left the hospital, knowing he must head straight for the Hall. What would happen when he got there? No, he blacked that thought out of his mind. He climbed on a bus, longing to overhear some sane conversation after the cross-talk of Bill and Charles. His seat was just behind two schoolboys with piercing trebles.

'That's a nice plane.'

'An ice plane? I've never heard of an ice plane.'

'A nice plane.'

'I never heard of a plane made out of ice.'

'I said a nice plane.'

'I know you did, you said an ice plane.'

'A – nice – plane.'

'No, you said an ice plane.'

'I didn't say an iced plane.'

'I didn't say you did say an iced plane, I said you said an ice plane.'

'I said an ice plane. I mean a nice plane.'

'There you are, you said an ice plane.'

'No, I didn't, I said a nice plane very quickly.'

'You didn't say a nice plane very quickly.'

'I did.'

'You didn't.'

'I did.'

'I never heard you say very quickly.'

'Anyway, I said a nice plane.'

'That's right. An ice plane. A plane made out of ice.'

'No, I didn't.'

'Yes, you did.'

'I didn't. I didn't. I didn't.'

'You did. You did. You did. You did. That's one more than you said, so you did.'

Jack felt as if he were travelling on an ice bus. The dialogue, so like a public exchange of letters between an author and a critic, had set his hands shaking.

Two buses, a number four followed by a number nine, approached.

'What's that bus?'

'It's a four.'

'No, it's a nine.'

'It's a four, look.'

'It's a nine.'

The number nine emerged from behind the number four.

'There, you see, it's a nine.'

'It wasn't before. It was a four.'

'You mean it's changed from a four to a nine? It was a nine all the time.'

'No, it wasn't.'

'Yes, it was. Yes it was for the last time. Seeya.'

And the winner-tormentor, swinging his satchel, ran down the stairs of the bus. Jack spoke aloud, but mostly to himself.

'I think there are enough mad people without trying to make more.'

Then he picked the bag off his lap and walked half a mile to the drive leading to the Hall. All the way up the drive he kicked the larger pieces of gravel, recently laid and sharp and dusty, his head full of a dream that he and Lorna would spend forty days and forty nights in the belly of the Hall simply staring at each other before beginning to move towards each other. He adjusted his black patch. As he neared the Hall, Lorna appeared on the long stone balcony wearing a tweed suit. She waved carelessly at him and pointed to a dandelion just before he trod on it. He changed the course of his foot in mid-air, nearly tripping. Lorna had plenty to say.

'What a beautiful day. I could even believe in fairies on a day like this, couldn't you, Jack? It's so marvellously summery, like being underneath a perfectly shaped blue bowl turned upside down. We must go for a walk. By the river.'

Jack put down his bag and followed her. He didn't much like her nature talk or the thought of being trapped under a blue bowl like a spider, but her subject-matter was less important than the notes of her voice, alternating pure and cracked sounds. As they walked he was fascinated by the size of her feet. He liked big feet. Her hair hung a good eleven inches down her back, yellow like the polished brass in a pub. He was afraid that its strands might be looped by the breeze and catch in the low, thorny branches which were beginning to close in on the path. It would have taken a tougher lad than Jack to destroy her little dialogues with wild flowers, a more sophisticated man to interpret her military bearing at their first meeting, her silences at their two hospital encounters and the country-girl twitter of today.

'Aren't you looking bright today?' she said, not to Jack, but to an obese brown bird. 'Come on, little one, won't you chirp chirrup for us?'

Attempting to enter her mood without faking it too obviously, Jack threw back his head and inhaled noisily.

'You should package this air and flog it in Blooter's,' he said. 'They'd sell it in the grocery department. Tinned air for invalids.'

Lorna stopped and looked at him, eyes big.

'I truly wish we could give it away, or some of it, to all the people who never have the chance to enjoy fresh air,' she said.

She snapped off a branch with her right hand.

'Isn't it perfect?' she asked.

Jack didn't know what tree the branch came from, let alone whether a forestry expert would class it as a good specimen or merely fair.

'What is it?'

'Why, it's pussy-willow, silly,' she said, tickled his cheek with one of its furry buds and skipped childishly ahead of him. He wanted to grab her from behind and squeeze his belly against her arse. The bud had excited a small sensual nerve in his face which was now pumping out frantic Morse messages to the rest of his body. He would remember that gesture. Perhaps pussy-willow had some special property. If so, there was probably good business to be done, exporting bundles of the erotically tipped branches to Hamburg. Hamburg, from what Jack knew of it, must have exhausted all the more obvious variations long ago, but pussy-willow might even surprise jaded directors of German pharmaceutical companies. He saw himself as skipper of a pussy-willow boat, steaming passionately through the oceans towards Hong Kong, city of Tiger Balm, where serpentine women lived for love alone, not brown birds and dandelions.

Lorna began to sing. She sang 'Greensleeves'. Jack had never met anyone who sang 'Greensleeves' outside of school. But her voice was pretty, perfectly tuned, slightly beaten-up, affecting:

'Alas, my love, you do me wrong ...'

Maybe I do, thought Jack, maybe I do wrong to cast you off so discourteously in favour of the unseen, fabled women of Hong Kong. Feeling contemptuous of himself, and gentle towards Lorna, he pushed away his grubby, golden imaginings and looked at her, trying to remember her for ever. Something small popped and squashed under his shoe. He stopped. For as far as he could see along the path, about a hundred yards, the ground was covered with minute frogs.

'Frogs,' he said. 'Shall we go back?'

'Of course not,' said Lorna, smiling. 'They won't do you any harm, poor little things. Just tread more carefully.'

She picked up one of the frogs.

'Look at it breathing so hard,' she said. 'Isn't it tiny?'

'I'd put it down. Frogs have cold blood and the temperature of your palm might be too much for it. It might burst into flames.'

He was trying to keep down the sick. Frogs were the unstoppably hopping, rubber creatures of his nightmares. He had trodden on one, and the little death buzzed in his head. Now she was holding one on her soft hand. Lorna faced him. He was, for a moment, sure that she was going to force the frog into his shirt or his trousers or his mouth and he began to shiver violently. But after one hard moment, her face softened and she put the frog down in some long grass.

'Hop away home,' she said.

'Where are they all going?'

A thought dark as a tadpole wriggled in his mind. Perhaps the frogs had come to meet him deliberately. Perhaps he was asleep. He stepped on another one, gagged and shivered again. If the pussy-willow had induced lust, the frogs were having the opposite effect. He could feel his cock shrivelling.

'Oh, here's a big one,' said Lorna.

Mercifully she didn't pick it up. But they had to stop to inspect it.

'What a fine, big old frog you are,' she said to it.

Jack couldn't look at it for long. Instead he watched, suspiciously, one of the smaller, less disgusting frogs leap on to his shoe and off again. He realized that on the sole of each of his shoes must be smeared the juice, if not the body, of at least one frog. He wondered how long it would be before he could manage food again. It was absurd. He could skin and gut rabbits. Frogs were different.

'I can't stand them at all. Let's go back.'

'There's nothing wrong with them. They do no harm. Those beautiful colours, all those different greens and yellows. Did you know they have teeth, little sets of teeth?'

'I don't mind the colours, it's their skins. It's the way they're soft and cold and hollow. And purposeless. They're no use.'

'But a little frog can't hurt you.'

'Of course not. They can't hurt you. Not your body.'

'Where else could they hurt you?'

'In your dreams.'

'All right,' she said. 'We'll go back. But we'll have to walk back along the froggy path. I was hoping we might swim.'

Jack walked carefully, trying not to brood on the swimming. They had no costumes, which would have been good. Except for the frogs. Or perhaps she had a costume under her tweeds. Soon they could see the Hall again and its formal lawn. It looked a good place, a frogless haven in a frog-ridden park. At the bottom of the lawn lay an artificial pond, too small to be called a lake. At its centre stood a Victorian woman made of marble, holding up a rusty brown sword. A few red goldfish flicked their way through the greening waters.

By the hall-stand, Lorna stopped and stroked her cheek with the pussy-willow branch.

'Daddy used to call me Pussy-willow,' she said, and watched his eyes, recording the automatic smile and then the twitch as he remembered where her father was. Not far away.

'I'm very sorry about him.'

'That's no use, it's a bit late, everyone's sorry I suppose, but—'

They looked at each other.

'Do you want to talk about him?' he asked.

'Not yet. We will. But no, it's not time yet.'

'Is your mother all right?'

'Yes, she's certainly all right, she's all right in Bath and Bath's all right if anywhere is. It's the right place for her. She's too old and timid to do anything. My mother has really retired. She's done nothing all her life, and now she's retired. I haven't.'

'I don't even know what you do.'

'I do what I want. I survive. I believe in surviving.'

'Hope we all do, but it's not so easy to do these days. You never know what bomb they're going to drop next.'

'I wasn't talking about bombs.'

She was tough now, she was a knife, cutting him up, slice by slice. He couldn't take much more.

'Lorna, be gentle with me. I'm not tough at all.'

She leaned against the wall.

'Are you scared of bombs? And scared of frogs?'

A kind of savagery took his mind.

'Anyone sane is afraid of the bomb. It can happen any bloody time. Growths and deep burns, light blasting out your eyeballs. Children. So I dream about frogs, but only from time to time. Mostly I dream about the bomb. You see, when I was fifteen I tried to imagine it, spent weeks working on trying to see it in my head. I couldn't see it all, nobody could. But I got some of the way, reading, looking at films and photos. I remember the bomb every day. Look, Lorna, I'll tell you a thing. To help you see it. Take all the books you like best, the most beautiful books you know. Choose a page at random in each of them and write across it: AT THIS POINT THE BOMB FELL. Then slash out the rest of the pages and burn them. Put – them – on a fire and burn them. That's something. That's something to do with the bomb. I'm not talking about book-burning, not talking about Hitler. There are thousands of people as bad as Hitler now. All the bomb people. I suppose what I did was a silly way of imagining. But it was something. A start.'

Lorna's eyes were excited, but she spoke calmly.

'You're not afraid of dying or burning, are you?'

'No, I'd sooner not survive the bomb. I'm sorry to be so bloody morbid. It might not happen. But it will.'

'Oh, it'll happen. Daddy used to say it would happen.'

'I read once that alcohol makes you more resistant to radiation and that cellars are the safest part of a house. So the survivors will probably all be the people who are lying dead drunk in cellars when it drops.'

'Would you like to see upstairs?'

He followed her. The staircase was dusty. Lorna's bedroom had been recently hung with photographs of English animals. There was a large, plain box of powder on her dressing-table and some china dogs. Then Jack noticed that between the frame of the bed and the floor was a wire mesh. Jack got down on all fours to look in the cage. Two small fox-terriers looked out at Jack. When Jack stood up, Lorna had removed the top half of her tweed suit, exposing a blouse which at first glance looked extremely expensive. She said:

'You know what they say in films?'

'They say all sorts of things—'

'They say: "I'll just slip into something more comfortable." And then they say: "No, don't bother to go out. Just turn your back." '

He did that, clasping his forearms in front of his chest. He felt disembodied, lighter than air. He found it hard to believe that he was still alive. He knew that he was unattractive, narrow-chested, big-nosed, skin too white, his eyes too pale, complexion marked over with a lot of small black spots and a few large red ones. He could make some girls laugh, but he hadn't had much real luck, apart from the fluffy-haired girl at the factory, strange, fumbling, almost speechless lust conferences in the store cupboard. But Fluffy was scared of getting up the stick. It had been better than nothing, much better than nothing. When Jack turned round, Lorna, wearing a long dressing-gown, was sitting on the bed.

She said: 'Come here, darling.'

Jack noticed that her lips were now scarlet, her mouth wider. Her voice had coarsened. She had decided to turn herself into a tart. Jack was hopeless the first time, coming when he was only half-way in. So they talked a little before he tried again. The second time was more valuable than the whole of Jack's previous life. By the time they'd had a meal, Jack was ready again. He stretched himself across the bed, arms reaching behind him. He felt almost entirely good as he aimed his chin at the ceiling, a melted man, with a new job – a servant with genital privileges. As Lorna cleaned his ears, he examined the blue American box from which she had taken the cleaning sticks. Q-Tips they called themselves, and the lid of the box bore a drawing of a Q-Tip. Q-Boats were boats which looked exactly like merchant ships but contained hidden fire-power. Jack read aloud from the box:

'The swab with the loving touch, added padding at stroking area makes it plumper, pillow-soft. Exclusive silkenized cotton – softest, purest made. Can't twist off stick. 100% sterile in convenient utility box. The stick with the gentle give, it bends under pressure yet is firm and steady in the hand.'

It also said, 'Used by more doctors and mothers', and 'The only cotton swab with safety-cushioned ends ... and flexible safety sticks.'

Lorna said: 'You laugh too much.'

As he began to laugh at that, she pushed her face slowly towards his, earwax-yellow Q-Tip held like a small spear in her right hand, breasts drifting over his chest like hot clouds. Jack stopped laughing, laughing seemed less important as she moved daringly about his body, the daughter of Tarzan on a climbing frame, as her teeth took his lower lip, as she chimed her breasts across his face, as she lurched backwards and he saw the white moon of her belly rise, as her hand touched and left him, touched and left him, held him as softly as – tightly as she knelt above him and most suddenly he was in her again and she was backing and forthing like a berserk railwayman heaving one of those levers which changes the points backwards and forwards and he thought of Hornby train sets and he was laughing away whatever she said or growled and now she was vacuum-cleaning him and he was holding on to the sides of the mattress, on a raft in a daft ocean, and heaving up his head to her and over they went in a lump of heat as he shouted rhythmically, 'The stick with the gentle give, give, give', until all heaven broke loose.

He muttered, 'Give me liberty or give me slavery,' and began to fall asleep. She pulled his hair until he sat up. Her eyes turned strange, as if supposed to deep-freeze or laser him, as she dressed and walked out of the room, which became totally stark as soon as it lacked her. Slap-happily, he pulled on his primeval jeans, shirt, socks and shoes and followed her.

As he pushed through the front door and ran into the drive, he saw she was sitting in a blood-coloured sports car, staring through the windscreen. He tried to get in beside her, but she'd locked the doors. He shouted invitations, orders, apologies for the orders, ingratiations, lullabies, inspirations, grovels, but for five minutes by the electric panel clock she stuck to her bucket seat without an answer on her face. Finally she moved, but not much, a twist of the buttocks, a twist of the ignition key, a shift to first gear. The car, surprisingly quiet, flowed down the drive at walking pace. Jack walked behind it, over the raked gravel. For a moment he saw her eyes in the driving mirror. Just before the drive opened into the road, she turned sharply on to the grass, smashing the vertical edge of the turf in four places. Jack followed. He had been so happy ten minutes before, but if he couldn't soon take some deep draughts of the special air between her shoulder-blades, he'd be sick. By now they were well clear of the trees which bordered the drive. Lorna's car suddenly accelerated, sliding across mown grass towards the roped-off cricket pitch, swinging away to the left, making a semicircle of bruised grass and heading straight for Jack. A sharp chromium bumper. Two vast glass eyes. Jack dived away to the right, but he dived too soon. Lorna corrected her aim and before she passed him he had to half-raise himself and dive a second time, a goalkeeper saving himself. The sweep of the car's wing blew over his face. He rose to see the car make another U-turn, knowing that with only one eye his distance-judging was all to cock. The car roared back for him. This time he faked a jump to the right, then dodged left, then had to scramble in order to keep his right leg. He knew he mustn't turn his back. The nearest tree was too far away. Worse than dodging a police horse. And at least with the cops you knew why they wanted to break your head. Next time she came at him, Jack waited till the last moment. Lorna smiled at him through the windscreen glass, specially strengthened glass, her face becoming larger, her smile wider. In searching that smile, in hoping that it would soon occupy the whole of her face instead of just her mouth, in concentrating on that smile, he either forgot to jump or decided not to. He was right. Luckily, the third time, at last, he had got it right. She stopped just in time, pushed open the passenger door and had one hand on his shoulder, one on his neck before he had settled beside her. She began to kiss his head, sometimes the top, sometimes the long back and sides, sometimes the front – his face. Then she relaxed against her door, repeated her smile, flicked open the glove compartment and poured him a whisky from a silver flask. He took small gulps as she leaned her arms and cheeks against the grey circle of the steering-wheel. For a moment he was shaken by whisky-anger, he was going to shout shit on your games, shit on your stupid games, shit on your velvety little life, shit on your cruel little class. Then he shook his anger down and drank again. Then she hit him.

He said: 'I love you.'

She barped the car's horn. She said:

'You're no damn use to me.'

'I want to stay. I was on my own.'

'Can't use you.'

'I'll do whatever you like. It's a big place. You need someone to help. Just for food. Any old job.'

'You bloody fool, is that the best offer you've got? It's a big place but I can buy more servants than I need – but I just don't happen to want all those slavey bodies cluttering up my property and spying on me. I don't want you hanging around my neck either.'

'But it's a big place. I could stick around the south-east wing or whatever and I'd only come out when you wanted me to come out.'

'Lemon curd, you're just so much lemon curd. I fucked you just now to see what you're made of and, believe me, you're lemon bloody curd all through. You can't do anything, can you?'

'Not much. I'm ordinary.'

'You bloody flatter yourself. You're just nothing.'

He didn't want to hit her now. He wanted to be part of her life for the foreseeable future. Because, for a few hours, she'd made him feel better than he'd ever felt before. And now he felt worse than usual, but that was much less important.

'You can stay,' she said.

'I'll do whatever you tell me to do.'

'Yes, you will.'

Everything was going according to plan.

Middle
1953-1963

Rodney at Oxford

Oh, Oxford University! Bulging udder, spouting intellectual teat! Sweet Gothick Spaceship! Adolescent Fever Ward! Gobi Desert Adventure Playground! Transylvanian Vault where hundreds of salaried Doctor Frankensteins create their monsters in the likenesses of Beowulf, Keynes, Rutherford, Happy Heisenberg, John (Tightarse) Dryden and all the Huxleys! Dust in the blood! Doom in the river! Suicide School! Succubus Centre! For Summer's here and the time is right for Twitching in the Street! Sherry-bellied, spike-walled, spire-spiked, Religioso Discotheque! Anti-Espresso Machine – all steam and no beans! Waiter, there's a university in my soup!

It wasn't the special freedom of Oxford which delighted Rodney. But there was a perfume of power in the air which made his nostrils expand. Deciding to become memorable, he bought six pairs of red rubber gloves at Woolworth's, wore them constantly and became a celebrity. People laughed at the red rubber, but since Rodney also wore Soustelle dark glasses, his wincing was not evident. He kept his room in heavy darkness, sliced only by three fierce, narrow-beam photographic spotlights. On his wall was a blow-up of Fatty Arbuckle, a choice with which nobody could argue. His friends, whether they could take it or not, were given brandy. Rodney's father was not only a newspaper editor, but a rich one, thanks to the laws of inheritance and the stock exchange. Rodney's decision to act a part and adjust his decor to suit that part was made urgently because he couldn't work out what the hell he was supposed to be. He never met anyone, except possibly Mike, who could have told him exactly what he was. So he made up a Rodney whom he sincerely loved. Certain things didn't quite fit. He wanted to be Rodney the Poet, despised by most, loved by the discriminating few. At first the few wouldn't print his poems. So he read their poems, was deeply moved by their tight-lipped approach to life and death, changed his style and began to see his poems in print. Nobody hated them, nobody loved them, but some people liked them enough to advise him how to become even more stylish. Most of this advice, because it was given affectionately, he took. The weather in which Rodney manufactured his poems was composed of comfort, dust and academic Muzak. Rodney was safely on his way.

Mike's job

One year and a half after Mike became a reporter on the Belston *Gazette* and three months after he took over the theatrical column on the same paper, his editor Barrett Brown, who by no coincidence was Rodney's father, took him out to dinner at the new chop-house.

Barrett I suppose this meal is really in lieu?
Mike Lieu?
Barrett I like the way you're dealing with the theatre generally. In general.
Mike Thanks. Thanks generally.
Barrett I wish I could give you more tangible encouragement.
Mike This is very tangible steak. I don't like steak usually, but this is very good.
Barrett I mean a raise or a bonus. You deserve one, in many ways.
Mike I wasn't looking for more money. My girl pays her own way. And the raise or rise is on its way, I suppose. When the union rate goes up.
Barrett Nobody could say you're not conscientious.
Mike I like most of the work. Except council meetings and taking the names at funerals. I wouldn't work as hard if I didn't like it. I'm not a fanatic for work as work. Though I may be a fanatic.

Barrett I'm glad to have you on the team. Let's have another half-carafe.
Mike Thanks. That's good.
Barrett It's very difficult ...
Mike Editing?
Barrett Explaining.
Mike Yes.
Barrett What do you want to do? In the long run.
Mike I'd like to write what I want to write.
Barrett Plays or something?
Mike Yes. No. I'm not sure yet. I'm young, people keep telling me I'm young, so I suppose I must be. I don't feel ready yet to write what I think I want to write. I'm trying to get ready. I'd like to write somewhere very open, where millions of people could see. Like I wouldn't mind being an Old Codger on the *Daily Mirror* if I could be a really honest Old Codger. And had lots of time for sorting out the questions.
Barrett That's right, Mike. Lots of time. I'm sure you'll do very well in whatever station, I mean field ... Look, I'll be frank.
Mike Can I be frank back?
Barrett Of course. It's very difficult ... I like your work, Mike – don't think I don't for one moment – but there's a certain amount of, not exactly criticism, not exactly negative response – I think the word would be disappointment.
Mike Yes? Yes. Well, I'm disappointed with myself a lot of the time. Are you disappointed with me?
Barrett Of course not. It's not me. Well, I can't evade some of the responsibility. But there is some disappointment.
Mike In the air? In heaven?
Barrett A little more solid than that.
Mike The owners? The directors? The theatres? The readers?
Barrett I'd be going beyond my brief to go into that, Mike, but you might bear it in mind.
Mike It's a bit general to bear in mind. It must be either the owners or the board of directors, which comes to the same thing. Or could it be the advertising department?
Barrett Ah, waiter, another half-carafe, please.

For six weeks, Mike bore it in mind. He spent longer on his

reviews and articles, but he didn't soften them. He avoided both drink and his editor. Then Barrett, with a sad face on, asked him out to dinner again. Mike could only manage an omelette this time.

Mike Do you think I'm getting any better?
Barrett I think you're doing very well in many ways.
Mike Let's have another carafe on that.
Barrett It's only that—
Mike Yes – how's the disappointment, then? Have they still got it? Is it getting worse? Is it like ivy gradually suffocating an oak or is it more like a clogged-up lavatory which has to be flushed?
Barrett They're still disappointed, I'm afraid. Disappointed with you. They think perhaps they made a wrong decision.
Mike I thought you made the decisions about me. What bothers them, anyway? Do I write badly?
Barrett No, Mike, of course you don't. Nobody thinks that. They don't say you write badly, or that anything's bad about you, but they do still feel disappointed.
Mike Well, if that's the case, I'm disappointed about them. You might tell them when you see them. If they are visible entities, of course.
Barrett Perhaps if, after I'd talked to you last time, you'd taken another tack in your reviews ...
Mike Tack? What other tack? I've been trying to go straight, straight as I could see. Wouldn't they be so disappointed if I tacked about all over the place? What disappoints these disappointed people?
Barrett It's hard to say exactly. Your approach, perhaps it's a question of your approach. In general.
Mike Too political?
Barrett Not at all, I'm sure they find your views very interesting, we all do, and after all, the *Gazette*'s not exactly dogmatic or hidebound one way or the other, is it?
Mike No, it's not one way or the other at all, it's right down the middle of the white line. And I just want to reassure you, I know it's not you, because you're a Liberal and hence a champion of tolerance, free speech and that. What bothers them?

Barrett I – er – you bother them.
Mike What I am, or what I write?
Barrett One can hardly separate them.
Mike One could try.
Barrett They didn't go into details. I'm sorry about all this. I think I know how you must feel. I hope you understand how I feel about this.
Mike I don't. No, I don't understand you at all. Who are *they*, anyway?
Barrett I can't go into that.
Mike Who are they?
Barrett I said, that's not at all how these things can be discussed. I can't possibly go into that. There's a way of doing these things.
Mike What are we doing? All right, I know. But you are speaking for *them*?
Barrett In a sense, yes.
Mike Pity they couldn't be here. Anyway, you can't go into details, right?
Barrett It's very difficult. You're not making it easy. I wish you could learn to take a hint like a gentleman.
Mike I'm a good reporter because I'm a lousy gentleman. And I'm a very disappointed reporter at the moment. You might pass that on and up. They want me to resign? That it?
Barrett They'd prefer you to. And I do have contacts on other papers. You'd have good references.
Mike 'Dear Sirs, I am extremely sorry to be causing you disappointment and I would like to offer my resignation, yours faithfully' – who do I send it to?
Barrett You don't have to write to anyone.
Mike I'm not going to.
Barrett What are you going to do?

Mike looked around the room. Two city councillors were hunched in plot over a corner table. An actress was staring into her own circular eyes in a circular mirror while her escort counted green pound notes. There were bank managers and a pensionable waiter. Mike picked up half a cold omelette and slapped it across Barrett's face, then stood up and poured red wine, very carefully, over Barrett's clean silver hair. He began to chant:

> 'Two-faced, crap-faced, liberal cunt.
> Two-faced, crap-faced, liberal cunt ...'

and allowed himself to be removed, non-violently but still chanting, by the old waiter, who had seen worse in his time. At the door, Mike turned around and shouted:

'Thank God I'm not a fucking gentleman!'

Barrett lowered his head and began to mop up with a starched napkin.

Mike's visit to the Registry of Companies was not disappointing. He discovered that James Devon, Jane Munche and Lorna Munche all belonged to the *Gazette*'s Board of Directors. So did Barrett Brown.

Until he was sacked, Mike had vaguely imagined, without gloating about it, that his income would gradually rise until his retirement. He had sensed that his standard of living would expand to meet his income, that he would move from plastic-encased sandwiches to frogs' legs by the end of his thirties, that he would eventually be granted a mortgage which he would swap for a higher mortgage, that he would insure his mortgage and that eventually he would own a house outright just in time for his funeral. Now he realized that he couldn't accept the basic conditions of the pattern, couldn't even make the down payment. He didn't qualify. As he grew older he became more cussed, spiky, bolshy.

Mike went into training for the future. He decided that the more property he owned, the freer he wasn't. He sold all his pleasure books and kept only those he needed for work, relying on libraries for entertainment. He rented a bad bed-sitter. He liked paintings, but several of his friends were artists and they gave him prints, drawings and even a couple of oils. His girls either cooked or were able to pay for his meals in restaurants. His unreliable income came from lecturing to evening classes and free-lance articles. He travelled by motor-bike. The bomb drove him into politics. Demonstration after demonstration, march after march, committee after committee, petition after petition – many of his friends became bored with the struggle, but Mike became more excited. Articles, speeches, demos, sit-downs, teach-ins, rave-ups occupied his years. When he was really broke he did a little thieving on the side. They never caught him.

Lorna and Jack

It was a matter of months before Lorna had broken Jack down into his basic components. Once he was lying in pieces all over the floor, she began to reconstruct him. But she put the bits together in a new way. She had used his imagination, the shaking passions of his long body, the gentleness of his mind and a programme of pills to burn him to the ground. Now she used the same tools to rebuild him. Before she came along, to push the metaphor, Jack was an asymmetrical house, home-made, added to eccentrically over the years, new rooms nailed on shanty-wise as they became desirable or necessary, a strange house certainly, but a house of open windows and pleasant surprises, walls at odd angles, doors which didn't fit too well but were good to walk through. Not a frightening house at all. There had always been a danger of fire. Push the metaphor. On the site where he once stood happily ramshackle, she excavated the ground and placed over the deep hole an iron shack without windows, a heavy padlock on the only door, a vulnerable shed, its inside walls covered with terrifying images of fire, its door painted with fire-coloured letters which said KEEP OUT. Metaphor ends.

Lorna was, perhaps, a great actress. A great actress is afraid of her part as she reads, rehearses, sways in front of that mirror, dresses, makes up. Then she plays the part, fearlessly.

Lorna knew all the dangers. Jack might turn round and strangle her. Slaves sometimes mutiny. His convoluted imagination might spawn a scheme so wild and complex that it would envelop and suffocate her like The Blob, a shapeless movie monster. For Lorna, The Blob was a combination of the Chinese people, semen and the working class. But she didn't waste many of her minutes being afraid. She woke up each morning, fought her enemies, slept again. She did not remember her dreams.

Was she beautiful? Sometimes, when she wanted to be beautiful. Her voice was sandpaper, rolls of velvet, corrugated iron, stinging nettles, rose petals, artichoke hearts in olive oil tinned and on the shelf – it all depended what she wanted her voice to do. She could sit in a room and force it to change colour to match her. Lorna.

An iced witch.

Raspberry pie with arsenic syrup.

An iron, body-breaking trap.

A cloud of plague.

The sweetest quim in capitalism.

The tightest.

She memorized the control panel at the back of Jack's brain, reached in blindfold whenever she felt like it and threw all the switches in the correct order. When Jack saw her sitting on her horse, she and the horse formed a picture which, to him, was of great religious significance. Sometimes she was simply an evil legend in his head. Often he wanted to shoot her.

Jack was kept busy. One afternoon he served lunch for both of them. She said nothing as they ate together, simply watched his successive plates to make sure he ate everything. When he'd washed up, she beckoned him to follow her upstairs. They made love twice, first briefly, then languidly. She even let him sleep for an hour, watching the clock until it said half past three. Then she woke him, gave him one of his special pills and showed him two cardboard boxes beside the bed. He hid his face in the pillow, afraid. He hadn't seen the boxes before, and by this time he was afraid of anything new.

It was so easy. She had been trained to own things. Soon she would own Jack completely.

'Have a look in the boxes, Jack.'

He half sat up and looked at them. White, glossy, bright cardboard. Neatly knotted up with string. One large white box, one smaller white box. One was bigger than the other. Shaped like cubes. Jack hurled his face back into the pillow and sobbed. Lorna considered whether to put the boxes away and produce them once a day, forbidding him to look into them until he screamed to be allowed to see. Impatiently she decided against it, that game would be fun, but quite unnecessary. He was so simple, so easy to eat. She brought the boxes and placed them beside him. By mistake the flesh of his back touched the corner of the larger box and he winced away. She put an arm round his shoulder and pulled him until he was sitting up. Her fingers moving in pink blurs, she undid the string from each box, then waited for Jack to remove the lids. He wouldn't. So she opened the large box and showed him the loudspeaker with its long coil of wire, opened the small box and showed him the microphone. He was still frightened. The loudspeaker was designed for the corner of some ceiling, its back was angled to fit a corner. Its face was metal, its mouth criss-crossed by small bars. It was dull grey. The microphone was stubby and silver.

'The loudspeaker goes in the shelter,' she said in one of her softer voices. 'You can take the ladder from the hall cupboard and fix the speaker in the corner of the shelter. Then you'll connect it to this mike. I'll have the mike beside my bed. Then I can call you when you're needed. Or just tell you things you ought to know.'

Jack began to nod his head. A good idea. Not a hard job. A good task, something he could do well. He wanted to please her. He said:

'And maybe, maybe you could play me, maybe I could bring your record player up here and you could play me music, down the mike, down the wire, through the loudspeaker and into the cellar, you know, when I move to the cellar when it's all ready. Music sliding down the wire—'

'Shelter,' she said. 'Not cellar. It used to be a cellar, but you're making it into a shelter, aren't you, Jackie?'

Jack grinned and wagged his head. The pill was working away in there, muddying his brain. His thoughts wallowed contentedly.

'Shelter. Yes. Shelter.'

'Yes,' she said. 'It's going to be our shelter. For the war. And you won't be frightened at all, will you, Jackie? You're going to turn it into the snuggest, safest little shelter in the world. And you're going to live down there, aren't you, Jackie, so you can keep it nice for both of us?'

He nodded, climbed off the bed and was reaching for his clothes.

'I'll come upstairs sometimes, won't I?'

His grin reappeared, anxiously.

'Sometimes, of course, sometimes. I'll need you, won't I, Jackie?'

She wobbled her body at him. He was approaching the stage where he could only understand blatant, cartoon gestures.

'Don't put your clothes on,' she said. 'It'll be better training for you if you don't. And I want to be thinking of you without your clothes on. Just take that speaker and fix it in the shelter. You don't need clothes for that. If you find it's cold down there, put on a pair of overalls. But nothing else. I'll be thinking about you, you see.'

'The overalls could be my uniform.'

'That's right.'

Jack stood still for half a minute, facing her, hoping she would say that she liked looking at his body, which she had said once before. But she shut her eyes against him, so he took the loudspeaker downstairs. When he'd gone, Lorna took her diary from the dressing-table. Each day was divided into squares like a school timetable. She looked at a square marked: 'J. It makes me lunch. It washes up.' She ticked that square. The next square said: 'J. Fuck it twice. Give it pills.' She ticked that. The next square said: 'J. Show it boxes. Let it fix speaker.' She added to the last sentence the word 'naked' in brackets. Then she ticked that.

Mrs Munche in Bath

A Saturday morning in Bath, that soft stone bowl for catching light. The air is blue, yellow and white. Mrs Munche and Dorothy walk up Milsom Street. Dorothy's face is over-powdered. Small flakes of lilac-scented powder adhere to the thin hairs of her face. She is tall, too rigid to be graceful. This is the way in which she has been taught to walk. She has been educated for a gentility which she cannot afford and which debars her from any productive form of work. She lives on a percentage of the profits produced by the men who tap rubber trees and on her polite salary as inefficient secretary to an animal charity. Dorothy looks through the other strollers on the pavement. Bath is her city. She smiles at her favourite shops. There is no hurry, the coffee table is reserved. Her stockings are pale, they will not droop, twisted into her new, unfussy suspender belt. Her high-necked dress is a mild orange and black, but predominantly black. Her hat, with its brief blue veil, is flattened to make her long face look shorter. Her petticoat hangs a little too low. It is beautiful, completely white and seething with lace at the hem; a present from Mrs Munche. Her brassière is small, pink, loose, unnecessary. From a necklace an heirloom ruby depends, swinging lightly against Dorothy's ribs. In one gloved hand she carries an oblong, embroidered handbag.

By Dorothy's side, Mrs Munche looks at everyone for half a second, wishing a small wish that she knew everyone in Bath, but knowing at the same time that her courage is too frail to withstand the shock of more than Dorothy and Dorothy's friends, who are all of them, in some way, slightly inferior to Dorothy. Mrs Munche, now with a sartorial tutor, wears Dorothy stockings and a Dorothy hat. Her bag is borrowed from Dorothy. She is bound in a tubular corset; her armour. Her shoes, white sandals which expose the upper part of her toes – toe cleavage – frighten her by their suggestion of nakedness, but

Dorothy approves of them at this time of year. They would be ridiculous in winter, of course. Dorothy is good at seeing snags, she has a strongly developed sense of the appropriate.

Dorothy in her orange and black, Mrs Munche in her pink and washed-out blue, are both appropriate to Milsom Street on a summer Saturday morning. They both note a student in jeans who is inappropriate. Mrs Munche dutifully records this judgment with a brusque thrust of breath down both nostrils. Dorothy signals her sympathetic distaste with the slightest lift of her chin.

It is the same every Saturday morning. Dorothy has never had a husband or children of her own and she is not a Lesbian. But she has shared a flat with a succession of timid ladies like Mrs Munche.

If, one Saturday morning, a hundred-foot-tall monster with a body of fire and a heart more powerful than a typhoon should rage down Milsom Street, the men who tap rubber trees would not even look up from their work.

Rodney and Lorna

Rodney could never have become a big, stamping poet. His imagination was his own, but it was a small field, much of it trampled into flatness or mud by the heavy shoes of schoolmasters. A wonder that he wanted to be any kind of poet at all, after being locked up in the marble Poets' Corner of his school English course. He had been shown Keats, his poetic mouth full of squashing, squirting plums. Keats, with the juice running down his chin and neck, staining his white body, like lung-blood. Keats, being arrested in a sub-tropical park of images by the critical police for exposing himself. Rodney had climbed the north face of Milton in mid-winter. He had made accurate engineering diagrams to illustrate the cogs and pistons of Popeand-dryden. Swift never threatened his sense of sense; he was never detonated by Blake. His English master was usually in a hurry because he wanted to arrive at Matthew Arnold's 'Dover Beach'. He liked to lead a class of thirty boys on to 'Dover Beach' and let them wander and ponder (note the rhyme). Then he would gather them all together and make a speech about the poetic scenery which surrounded them. It was for their own good. Rodney liked this. Matthew Arnold seemed to encourage him, personally, like some ghostly great-uncle or cricket coach:

'Now, nobody's going to say I was a great poet. No, no, my boy, don't flatter, I know you know. I wasn't great, but if you're looking for a good solid minor poet, a number six for your second eleven – Arnold's the name. Minor, certainly, but just you try to run an anthology of nineteenth-century poets without me. Go ahead and try. Limitations, yes. But I knew those limitations. Rodney, my boy, take my advice. Settle for being a good minor.'

That, by the end of his second year at Oxford, was Rodney's decision. He not only recognized his limitations, he respected them, declined to look beyond them even when they appeared to be closing in on him. As athletes train by puffing round frosty parks or heaving black weights towards the ceiling, so Rodney would pant his way through a Spenserian sonnet or heave heavenwards line after line of exhausting ballade. He kept his poems small, and the editors, to whom he sent them in strict rotation, enjoyed their modesty or cowed quality. They were reliable, as if stamped 'Made in Oxford'. When Rodney wrote his sonnet 'Christmas At Home', for instance, it began with a light irony which suggested that everyone really hates Christmas at home. Then, with the smoothest change of gear, he reversed this feeling until a mildly warm Christmas-at-home atmosphere descended, only slightly chilled by the implied hint that the reader was rather shallow to have accepted so unquestioningly the apparent cynicism of the opening. Rodney was celebrating this poem's publication in a Cambridge magazine, alone, with a brandy, under one spotlight, when Lorna entered his room without knocking.

There was a three-second double-take on Rodney's part. She

was mostly in darkness, but the spotlight was snarled in her bright hair. Rodney remembered the hair first and then the girl. For a moment he thought she'd come to knife him. But her smile was shy as she introduced herself and asked him out for a drink. He went nervously, extremely conscious that while he was wearing a smart charcoal suit, she wore a rough sweater, slacks and hair dangling all round her head. As he observed the two of them walking together, he knew that everyone must think that such a bohemian–businessman combination could only end in cold blood, cold sweat or chilly tears. They sat on leather bar-stools which sighed beneath their arses. Her voice was soft but fast. Sometimes she failed to finish sentences, veering between domination and fits of nerves.

'Martinis, please, the American kind, you know, nearly all gin,' she told the barman, a pale old man whose main interest was rabbits, about whose diet he was writing a monograph in his considerable spare time. He had fed his rabbits experimentally on unbelievable permutations of chemicals, vegetables, drinks, meat, fruit, pudding, mash and mush, and had conscientiously recorded their reactions, which varied from malnutrition to satisfaction to delirium and, occasionally, death. He himself had never read a monograph, and his *Rabbit Diets of All Kinds* had got completely out of hand, running to about 200,000 words.

Rodney said:

'Don't think I've ever had a Martini.'

She laughed.

'You must practise. It's nearly all chilled gin. It clears your throat and oils your mind. You can be almost anything if you keep wearing suits like that and drinking Martinis, you can. Look, I can slob around in any old thing, there's nothing much I want, being rich, but if *you* want something ... Some men glum around in brown tweed with great bags in it, all their pockets full of rubber bandages and half-dead cigarettes and forms they can't quite finish filling in. Their breath, you know about their breath, it's a brown tweed cloud of beer, always beer; even if they drink whisky their breath keeps that brown smell. But the boys who cut right through to the artichoke heart, their cheeks are smooth like good writing paper, cream-laid, their suits are black, their breath smells keep clean (they've been drinking Martinis), the insides of their mouths are cool. Like caves. And they can become tycoons. Or werewolves. Or Eiffel Towers. Or they can choose to be dead. Whatever they like, because it's a magic drink. Transmogrifying.'

Rodney, who was embarrassed by women, was upset by all this talk about the inside of men's mouths.

'It's so easy for you, Rodney. It's going to be so easy. You look good, strong face, you haven't got those cadaverous dips in your cheeks, and your body's strong too, I should think; you've got a mind with all its lights switched on, your daddy's rich and your ties are good-looking, you could go anywhere, take any job, mix with anyone. I bet you're a good mixer.'

Rodney couldn't answer. She looked at him closely, moved so that her arm was pressing her sleeve against his sleeve, which pressed against her arm. Through the two sleeves his arm felt the shock of her arm. It was an absurdly second-hand sort of contact, he thought, but the erotic nervous messages were shooting round his shoulder and down his body nevertheless. He asked:

'How did you know where I'd be? I mean, why should you want to see me at all?'

She ordered more Martinis and looked into the fresh glass as if it held the answer to a great deal of pain.

'I was on my own, travelling home to be on my own, and I thought I'd like to see someone I knew. But my friend wasn't in. She was the one who first showed me your poems.'

'Oh, you've read—'

'Wasn't going to. I started to read this poem, then I saw your name, then I remembered and thought it must be you. Well, I stopped, but then I had to start again. Those words were so gentle, so insistent—' she was talking crap of course, but it was honey-flavoured crap, 'and I've read everything you've published since, and Rodney, I believe in you. No, I shouldn't have said that.'

She lowered her head as if she were blushing, as she well might at such a hammy performance, took her drink and downed it. Rodney ordered two more.

'I'm not sure that I believe in myself,' he said. Then he had to find six shillings to pay the rabbit expert before starting again. It sounded worse the second time.

'I'm not sure that I believe in myself. Some days I feel I know *exactly*' – and he squashed his fist on the bar to underline the word – 'what I am and what I should do. But sometimes—' sip, sigh – 'I feel I'm just one more animal in a disorderly, inexplicable zoo. Well, not quite an animal—' laugh, sigh – 'I mean, I don't feel like eating people or anything. No, I so often feel so pointless.'

She moved her eyes from side to side of his face, as if caressing it.

Now they were in a punt, moored in a green-smelling backwater, her hand among his hair. She was saying:

'But perhaps you wouldn't feel so pointless if you knew what you were going to do when you left Oxford.'

Rodney, clutching his knees to hide his hard-on, muttered the word 'journalism'.

'But aren't you saying that just because Mike's a journalist?'

'Maybe. Maybe you're right.'

'But you're nothing like Mike.'

They were sitting in an oak-panelled hotel dining-room.

'Rodney, I've been talking to Tom Wilkinson about you. He's starting a new monthly called *British Letters* and he wants an editorial assistant. He likes your poems and he wants to meet you.'

Rodney clasped his hands together and shook his head a few times. Marvellous. He stared at nothing, letting the brightness of the cutlery form a pleasing blur.

'I'd like to meet Wilkinson. I read his poems – *The Lighthouse in the Forest*, that's a tremendous collection.'

The wedding

The Revd Realeigh, small black suitcase in his right hand, the ecclesiastical equivalent of the doctor's magic bag, plodded halfway up the steps to the Hall and then stopped. Jack, in a blood-red open shirt, overalls and bare feet, lurched out to meet him with a wide smile, clutched him by the shoulders, laughed a sort of wordless greeting, then turned to escort him through the main door and into the study. The curtains were drawn, a powerful bulb shone through a heavy crimson shade. All furniture had been removed except for the late Colonel's desk and a plain sullen brown table. On the table glowed a comprehensive selection of whisky, vodka, gin and mixers. In front of these bottles stood four baroque goblets of red, white and clear Venetian suggestiveness. The Revd Realeigh, always suggestible, immediately became occupied with a mental picture of a moustached Victorian gent in evening dress reclining under the weight of a bubble-curled, Lorna-shaped nude, while a blindfolded violinist induced his instrument to squeal exquisitely.

Jack picked off the desk an eighteen-inch crucifix and handed it to the clergyman, who asked:

'Where did she find this? It's a strange, um, style, isn't it?'

'Strange? Wouldn't say that. Strange, what's strange?'

'The style, I suppose. The figure is, er—'

'That man on it? That's Jesus, you see.'

'Yes, of course. One would hardly make a carving of anyone else being crucified, would one? But he's made out of such a worn kind of wood, with, well, wormholes, and such rough limbs, like an object that's been used too much, a piece of wood that's been washed around a beach a great deal, by the sea, you know.'

'Used, yes. Yes?'

'And the cross itself. Most unusual.'

'Mm.'

'It's the black wood of the cross perhaps, the way it's made. It looks more like iron than wood, as if it's been made in a factory. As if it's very efficient.'

'Oh, that's right, that's very good, as if it's been made in a factory for making crosses, yes, you almost look for the trade-mark, the manufacturer's name on the back, don't you? Design Centre Award?'

'But why's he smiling?'

'Because it's over.'

The Vicar looked up, straight into Jack's smile.

'It's not supposed to be funny, is it?'

'I don't know.'

'Where did it come from?'

'I made it.'

'Then did you mean it to be funny?'

Jack walked away from him, shrugging alternate shoulders. He turned, making a long, loose gesture with his right hand.

'Not just funny. I don't know. I bet there were plenty of people laughing at crucifixions. I don't know. Was Jesus meant to be funny? I mean, was Man meant to be funny?'

'I hardly think so.'

'But that's the way it fucking turned out.'

'I hardly think so. To me, Man still retains, even at his most debased—'

Jack had brought a miniature Victorian mirror to within eight inches of the Vicar's nose. Over the surface of his own tired face, the Revd Realeigh noted a shining, thin skin of sweat. His mind had not been on the argument; he had been worrying over Lorna's bared body in his head, occasionally distracted by the necessity of answering Jack. As reliable as Pavlov's poor old dog, the Hall invariably brought him a severe attack of lust.

His discomfiture was only increased by the arrival of the bride and groom. Rodney, in his black suit, was extremely drunk. Lorna was wearing a Victorian nightgown of lace, yellowed with age. The skin of her body showed through the painstakingly embroidered holes. Before the Vicar could begin the service, Jack screwed up his face, ran out of the door and crouched at the bottom of the cellar steps, head jammed between his hands. Then the Vicar began:

'Dearly beloved brethren . . .'

Jack on the cellar stairs

It would be good to have a spiral staircase in a tent. Old ladies hate stairs. Someone has invented a kind of lift for them which hitches over the banisters and zooms them up to the top or down to the bottom, depending on whether they are at the top or the bottom to start with; they have to sit sideways. They advertise those things with bad black-and-white drawings on the backs of magazines. A staircase is a machine. Very primitive kind of machine. It's unlucky to pass anyone on a staircase, Jacob's Ladder or the Odessa Steps. Cinderella ran down the steps because she was late, she built a stairway to paradise, but Dorothy Maguire was the deaf-mute at the bottom of it waiting to be strangled, waiting for her neck to be spiralled like a staircase. Staircases in dolls' houses are absurd. If I had a staircase I wouldn't carpet it, I'd buy a load of sand, spill it at the top and let it drift down like a waterfall. A dry waterfall. Yellow. Silver. Or maybe, maybe build small channels either side of the stairs like gutters, connect them to a tap and have a permanent indoor wet waterfall. If I had a family and lived in a bungalow I would forbid anyone to use the word 'stairs'. Or 'upstairs' or 'downstairs'. The Man Upstairs is meant to be God. Who is the Man Downstairs? Me. Cellar steps. Stay down. The dark at the top of the stairs. I've seen a perfect miniature staircase in a joiner's window. I suppose every apprentice has to make one. They lead nowhere. Look, I'm sane enough, I'm sane enough to sit here and concentrate on the subject of stairs to keep my mind off what the hell's going on upstairs. Stairs. Continentals have stairs on the outside of their houses, sometimes. As I was going up the stair, I met a man who wasn't there. How many people have died on stairs. Must have been a lot, including all those run through by Zorro and the Three Musketeers only there were really Four, I know. Detectives are always climbing stairs in films. So are lovers. Yes. Airliners keep their stairs on wheels.

You can make a rope ladder by using knitting needles as rungs. Ladders don't count. Lifts are completely different. I am now at the bottom of the stone stairs. Stone, stone, stone. But I won't go up them, not unless Lorna calls me on the speaker. I can hear her shouting now, but she's shouting at Rodney. I'll be here if she needs me, waiting on the stairs.

Jack's letter to Lorna

Dear Lorna,

I want to explain. When you and Rod went off on your honeymoon, I thought it was a bad moon. You left me loose in the Hall. Lorna, sometimes you make me like a prisoner, and sometimes you leave me all free, it is all booms and slumps. I went into different rooms, but there was nobody to tell me what to do, so in each room I just stood there and looked around and didn't know anything. Oh yes, in the kitchen I ate three bowls of cornflakes. In your bedroom, I went in there, I looked out of the window. It all looked green out there. I took thirty pounds I found, it was the first time I touched money in a year, wasn't it? I read the words and the numbers on the money for a bit. I told the money it was my wages because I needed wages. Then I got on a train. I didn't know what pills to take and I couldn't find my usual, so I took two different pots of pills.

I got to London and thought about a lot of things. I thought about my heart first, I know it is a machine for pumping blood and it does that quite well and I admire my heart for that. All the same I wish it was simple like a Valentine heart.

You know I like surprises, well, so I was pleased when the double-decker bus I was on top of hit the Ministry of Power smack between the porticoes. Had a good view, only a bit of a jolt and a black eye and of course I laughed all the way downstairs. Men came out in suits and stood round the bus-driver. He was even happier than me, and he was looking for a lavatory, he was drunk. I started to interview the bystanders, pretending to be a reporter, but the Ministry men kept saying they could say nothing so I walked into the Ministry and found the press office, well, in a way I suppose I was looking for Mike because I thought he might have a job reporting in London still and I still wanted to see him despite all the bad things you told me he did to people. In the press office there was just a brown tray on the floor with cups full of brown tea. There was nobody in the room to tell me what to do, so I looked out of the window on to a roof and there was a naked girl. Sunbathing girl. Then I had a feeling about the ceiling that the ceiling was going to fall on me so I ran out of the Ministry of Power and found a brand-new cigarette on the pavement which was the third lucky thing to happen to me, so I decided I was born lucky, even if some things have gone wrong.

Then and there on the spot I decided to become an actor. I made a lot of gestures with all my limbs and I made booming noises with my stomach. I spent several days trying to get a job acting but the nearest I came to it was when I was taken home from a pub by this Duchess who had a very rich carpet. I saw my shadow on the carpet. The shadow was big. There were woven birds and fishes of all kinds inside my body shadow. She told me that only £55 had been contributed for the Mausoleum of Empress Eugenie and £50,000 was needed and I said I thought that was fair enough, but she didn't like me, that Duchess I mean, because I kept getting visions and every time I have a vision it hurts and it means less days to live.

I was in the street, the Strand, and a lot of clouds started to come down the sky like visitors from other planets. I thought if they are visitors from other planets they have plenty to cry about. I thought about a lot of things. Thought of cyclists and how their feet go round and round taking them to places where they could never afford to live. I thought of all those miners getting those diseases, and noises underground and those groups of people above ground all crying like clouds. I thought about a man I saw who had a goitre like some people have beards. I thought about sad women cooking badly till they put their best pillows into the gas ovens and poison themselves with gas, you know how they do. Kept thinking about you, though, and you seemed real and all the others were just in my head, I think. I get all these dreams growing out of the top of my head like hair. Sometimes my hair hurts, did I ever tell you?

I went down Fetter Lane and there was an old man crying. That was in the afternoon.

Then there was another afternoon. I walked down the Mall and it was pink-coloured, like blood and water mixed and frozen up. It was like deep pink ice and I could see down through it, to somewhere under the ice. And down there there were two black stones but then they were the eyes of some old soldier in this frosty greatcoat and so I asked him questions about the next war and what it would be like and then he opened his mouth to speak to me, but all that came out was the noise of gunfire. And then the Household Cavalry came along and trampled over his bit of ice.

I know a lot of this doesn't make sense, but I want you to know what's been happening not just to my body, but to my head as well. As I write this I suddenly find that the whole of the top part of my body is tense as if wire was pulling it tight, including my neck and head. I'm sweating. There are birds making sad noises in the sky, like radios. I sometimes feel like a wall with a slogan painted on saying something I don't agree with.

There are a lot of things. My eyes only like a few of the things they see. All over my hands are little lines which I don't understand. Some people think they know what lines on hands mean. I don't think they know at all. I have eyebrows to keep the sweat out of my eyes. I make up talk in my head. Sometimes I just go around hitting solid things, because I wish I was solid. I wish I didn't know anything about anything. But I know a little. In London I keep shouting under my breath. Just now I was comparing myself to a jellyfish and the jellyfish came off best. Joke.

Lorna, this is later. A day later I think. I'm writing this later anyway and hadn't meant to. I saw Mike across the road in Soho so I ran away. I thought a lot since I started writing this letter about why I came away. I thought I wanted to try being free. I was silly. I can't do it and I don't want to do it. It took me ten minutes walking up and down just now before I could go into a shop and buy a box of matches because I was afraid to talk to the person behind the counter.

Lorna, I'm sorry I ran away. Will you come and get me? My address is on the back of this envelope. I am nearly dead and these are the wrong pills. Please come and get me quick.

Yours, JACK

Mike's broadsheet

In June of 1960, Mike was given a duplicating machine (hand-operated) by a friend whose magazine had just collapsed. There was nothing to do but start a broadsheet of his own. He called it *Overthrow*, edited under the name of Klaus Mauser, wrote it all himself, never deposited a copy in the British Museum, advocated disruptive illegal action and flogged it for whatever he could get at demonstrations. *Overthrow* wasn't popular. For some long-term peace-lovers it was too unscrupulous. For some socialists there were too many gags. The fastidious found it messy, although it was technically remarkable considering the means of production; anyway, fuck the fastidious.

Even the peace movement, which trusts its children, began to distrust Mike as a maverick. You never knew where he was. He had stopped recording how much he owed, except to friends. Years before, he'd stopped recording the money he'd lent to other people. He cut down his possessions even further and opened up his life. For travel, he had a succession of motor-bikes. For living, he had an attic, just like Jack in the old days. He thought of Jack often, wondering if he was still at large. He kept a weather-eye on Rodney's career, but from a distance. Lorna was not in his mind, but in the far past. There had been many girls. Mike was attractive to women but not very good with them. He couldn't concentrate on a relationship. His mind was always whizzing off in different, usually political, directions.

Jack's recurring daydream

As he shuffled the cards for the ninth game of patience that day, sitting under the brightest light in the cellar-shelter, alone, Jack began the excited *sotto voce* commentary with which he usually enlivened these games:

And it's welcome back, viewers, to the Shelter Club, and as you can see, Jack is just mixing them for another attempt to complete a Seven-Up Patience, and, while he shuffles, Rodney is once again fixing the size of the stake with him, but we won't be sure what it is until they press their stake buttons and the amount goes up in lights. And there it goes! Rodney has bet two thousand against one thousand that Jack won't make out with this particular hand. And now Jack's starting to lay them straight, there they go, one, two, three, four, five, six of the best face-downwards and one face-up – it's the three of clubs – one, two, three, four, five face-downwards on top of the first row, and one face-up – seven of spades – one, two, three, four downers and one up – jack of hearts, lucky for Jack – one, two, three down and one up – two of hearts, that'll be across and on to the black three in a few seconds for the first turnover – one, two, down, one up – four of spades – one down, one up – yes, that's the first ace up, ace of spades – and one up – it's another ace, ace of hearts and so that gives us the complete layout, two aces to go up straight away and a certain turnover of three. And there they go! And that's a nice turnover – three of hearts, four and five of spades. So the three'll go up on the ace and two, and what's underneath that three? Ten of spades, right over on to the red jack. And the next turnover gives him the four of clubs. That gives him his first dupe, first duplicate – four of clubs and four of spades – and a dupe's never good news, but Jack's had a good run in before he even takes the pack and Rodney's not looking too happy with that first run. Jack's breaking into the bulk of the pack now, those of you who don't know the game should watch how he has to deal the cards by threes into his other hand, always taking the first card of any three and the first one doesn't help him now, but it will later – that's the king of hearts. Next three, and it's another ace! Ace of clubs and that gives Jack three aces up before he's done a single run through the pack. Card underneath the ace is no use, so it's on to the next three. Ten of hearts, no good. Sorry, ten of diamonds, that was the ten of diamonds. 'Nother three. No, it's the other black seven. Clubs. Now it's a red seven, no. Black five, no. Here comes one, yes, two of diamonds, fits neatly on to the three of clubs and from under the two comes the ace of same, ace of diamonds to give Jack four aces up in a row and that can't be bad on his first single run through the pack, and the deuce diamond goes up on the ace and under the ace there's a black jack to go on the red queen, so that's a one-two-three boost for Jack. Last three of the first single run and it's the six of diamonds, nice, fits on the seven of spades and can be topped by bringing over the five of spades, and here we go, because under the six is the four of hearts and down it goes on the black five and over comes the three of clubs leaving an empty row for the first king, wherever he may be lurking. Oh, and the three of diamonds was under the four of hearts, so that goes down on the ace and deuce. Turnover in lane four, and it's the nine of diamonds, moves over on to the black ten in lane three. Turnover, and it's the two of spades, up on to its own ace, leaving a second open lane for another king. And that's the end of the first single run and Jack must be hoping that the complete double run will be as strong as that. So far he's cut pretty successfully into the deep, that's what we call the end lane with the six face-downers, and he's got four aces up with only one dupe to his name. Here goes on the second single run. Nine of hearts, no. Nine of clubs with nowhere to go. What he needs is a king now. Six of clubs, *nada*.

And there's the first one, king of spades. Down it goes in the empty row one and over comes the red queen plus her jack. Turnover, and it's a nice one, five of diamonds, the four of spades moves over from row five to give Jack another turnover. And it's another black king, clubs. Will he put it in the open lane or hang on for a red king? Yes, up it goes. Turnover, black nine, could be good if he grabs a red eight soon. Back to the pack and it's a queen who's black, she'll have to stay there a while. Next a black jack to bring the first double run on an end. Not bad going at all, Jack seems to be sweating a bit, but I don't think Rodney's got much sweat left in him, don't forget that he stands to lose two thousand, Jack only stands to pay out a thousand. And Jack begins another run through the pack – king of hearts, and I bet he's sorry to put up that second black king now, but that's the game. Ten of hearts – fits neatly on that black jack and the nine of spades comes over – turnover – and it's the king of diamonds and that's a welcome sign for Jack and a warning sign for Rodney. Black eight from the pack, down it goes on the nine of diamonds. Jack of diamonds shows in the pack, but there's no home for him yet a while. Seven of hearts – over on to the eight of spades. And there, right under that red seven, there's the queen of clubs. Down she goes on the king of diamonds, over comes the red jack and it's – Turnover Time! Six of hearts, well, that means the five of clubs can come out of the pack and into the game. And the jack of spades completes the first half of the second double run through the pack, but the jack of spades is spare at this stage of the game. Second half of the second double run and it's the nine of hearts, no. Nine of clubs, nothing. Ten of diamonds and it looks as if Jack has struck a bleak patch – jack of diamonds and *that* won't work either. That's the end of the second double run and here we go again with the odds really building up against Jack now. What he badly needs now is a red eight and a black six to give him a couple of turnovers. King of hearts, but there's no open space for him. Black six, there's the black six I said was needed, and it's clubs and down it goes on the seven of hearts, over comes the five of diamonds and once again it's Turnover Time! And what does he get? The ten of clubs, possibly the most useless card he could have turned up at this stage. Seven of clubs – no. Jack of spades again, and there's still nowhere for him to go. Pick up the pack and here we go again! And that's more like it, nine of hearts, plonk it goes on to that black ten and under the nine there's the four of diamonds. That fits neatly on the five of clubs. Nine of clubs, no. Seven of diamonds, no. And that old jack of spades again, and no again. Jack's getting down to the bone now, this looks like a hard one to crack and Rodney's smiling now, no doubt in *his* mind about how it's going to turn out, or rather *not* turn out. Into the pack again – king of hearts, no. Nine of clubs, oh no. Seven of diamonds, uh uh. Into the pack again, and it's a slim pack now. Five of hearts and Jack stops. Something he can do. He takes his three of clubs over on to the four of diamonds, puts the four of hearts thus exposed up on to his ace, one, two, three and tops it up with the five. Well, that may not save the day, but this is one of those games in which you never say die until you're dead. Back to the pack, black seven, no. That old familiar jack of spades, still waiting hopefully for his queen. King of hearts, no. Jack of diamonds, no. Jack of spades, no, how many times have we got to tell him? Black nine, red seven, black jack – not a sausage. Red king, red jack, black jack – no. Looks like the finish. Yes, I think it is. Yes, there it is, with eight cards still on the board not turned over and seven more still obstinately sitting in the pack, that's the sorry end of another bid and Jack's giving his familiar rueful grin as he hands over a bundle of a hundred tenners to Rodney. And they seem to be conferring, maybe there's another big bet coming up. Yes, Rodney's nodding his head and they're moving over to their buttons, and there it goes, yes – Rodney's bet Jack four thousand to two thousand that he can't make out in yet another session of Seven-Up Patience. And here we go again ...

Eating plaice

This is how Rodney eats a plaice. Between his knife and fork, he overbalances the fish and scrapes away every blue-black particle of mackintosh skin. Then the point of his knife follows the line of the spine, removing the good cream flesh to an eating pile at the side of his plate. This process is repeated on the top side. Skin-and-bone debris are transferred to Rodney's bread-plate. Rodney clicks his fingers and a fresh bread-plate is brought. All unpleasantness now removed from the table, Rodney begins to eat. Slowly, contentedly.

Jack eats more messily. Ideally he would always eat with his fingers. He always does so when he eats alone, which is nearly always. Knives and forks are machines and he's not fond of machines. Besides which, he dislikes the taste of metal and appreciates the salt deposits of his own fingers. So Jack, alone, takes the plaice to pieces manually. Good finger-licking. He eats too quickly. He tends to fart afterwards.

Mike only eats plaice because it's good for him. Such food reminds his tongue of soap. Meat reminds him of worse things. He prefers food which rouses no such images of blood or dead flesh – eggs, for instance, and clean-limbed breakfast cereals.

It's all the same to Lorna. Lorna will eat anything.

It should be remembered that of these four, only Jack has ever gone for a week without a cooked meal, and Jack has only once shown even the slightest symptoms of malnutrition. Mike and Jack, in their different ways, are both conscious of the privilege of never having starved. Mike is slightly ashamed of it. Jack is glad of it. Rodney talks about cooking, but doesn't care about food. Lorna sometimes sees the oceans and rivers of the globe as convenient extensions of her estate.

Three of Jack's dreams

A salvationist is addressing a meeting. He produces and spreads on a polished table a set of Salvation Stamps. They can be bought for whatever you care to give. Jack picks one up. It is beautifully printed, far finer and more expensively produced than any postage stamp. Immediately the salvationist points to Jack as a man who has made his decision, and calls upon him to announce how much he'll pay for the stamp. It seems like the first stage in a salvation auction. Jack refuses to buy, throwing the stamp back on the table. He explains that he is merely interested in the stamps, not in buying salvation. He suddenly senses, in the people around him, a bulging wave of anger.

Jack is at a table and frogs are served. Jack is with a gourmet, who licks his lips. The gourmet explains the latest technique in the cultivation of frogs' legs. Three of the frogs' legs are taken off and the frog is left alive. It can hop on the one leg and is now, explains the gourmet, what is technically known as an orthopod, or one-footed animal. The frog grows three more legs, which are in turn removed. Jack sees the legs being taken off, they come away like the legs of an overcooked chicken. There is no blood, although the frog is alive. Then Jack sees a large toad with two blunt, gristly horns.

Jack sees a girl so beautiful that he is immediately in love with her and cannot bear to let her out of his sight for a moment. She goes into a ladies' lavatory, and he follows her just in time to see her shutting her cubicle door and locking it. But he can't bear to wait outside, he must go in and see her straight away, pissing or not, or he might lose her. Without thinking that the door might be bolted, he decides instantaneously to put a coin in the cubicle door's slot and open it. But he feels a penny would be unworthy of the beautiful girl in the cubicle. So he puts a half-crown in the slot.

But most of Jack's dreams are something to do with the bomb.

From a radio interview with Rodney

Interviewer How old were you when you began to write poetry?
Rodney About ten. I noticed that Robert Browning had the same initials as myself, so I read his complete works. They left me dissatisfied. I decided to see what I could do myself.
Interviewer Did Oxford influence your writing much?
Rodney Quite the reverse.
(*Interviewer laughs.*)
Rodney I treated Oxford as a mistress should be treated. As a springboard.
Interviewer Continuing your metaphor, where did the arc of your dive coincide with the water?
Rodney (*laughs*) In the somewhat over-chlorinated deep end of London literary life. Tom Wilkinson, to whom I owe so much, accepted a sonnet sequence, summoned me to Kensington and offered me a job at twenty pounds a week. I was put in charge of Hopeless Cases, rejecting about two thousand poems in two years.
Interviewer It was Wilkinson who published your first collection – *Ivory* – wasn't it?
Rodney He was so kind.
Interviewer A beautifully produced volume.
Rodney Certainly the designer had a field day.
Interviewer I prefer your later work, actually.
Rodney It is certainly more recent. And more inhibited. I'm glad to say. The currently fashionable notion that poetry should be unfettered is slightly distressing. I like wearing tight, well-tailored clothes, a strictly knotted tie, and so forth.
Interviewer And this preference for formal verse coincided with the policy of *British Letters*?
Rodney Certainly, but in some aspects my tenure there was a mistake. I think it hardly right that a poet should immerse himself in literature as a profession. The cult of the amateur

never had a more rabid devotee than myself – the craftsman amateur, you understand ...

Interviewer How should a poet make his living?

Rodney You mean, a poet who lacks a private income? I was about to tell you. After *British Letters* I moved to Multicolor Advertising, shortly after my marriage. This I found rather more suitable.

Interviewer You found no clash with your principles?

Rodney Certainly not. The salary was excellent. I was never called upon to write copy for products which I considered vulgar. My short but intense hours in the office keyed me up for longer hours in my study, refining my verses. Finally I decided that public relations formed the most fruitful field for me. So I moved to Global Image, a very going concern. And I'm very happy there, thank you.

Interviewer Are you working on a new collection at present?

Rodney I am working on two poems at the moment – a villanelle about Martin Buber and a sixteen-line sketch of Pollensa, a pleasantly dowdy town in the north of Mallorca. I am also writing a monograph on the songs of Schubert.

Interviewer I wouldn't associate you with Schubert.

Rodney Thank you. It is basically a hostile monograph, stopping just short of a sneer.

Interviewer Who would you say had influenced your writing?

Rodney Rilke, Addison, Li Po and Trollope. That's what I always say.

Interviewer And what do you think the function of a poet in society should be?

Rodney Decorative?

Mike switched the damn thing off and turned to the girl whose article he was trying to type. He said:

'Jenny. What's Global Image?'

'Don't know. But I know who will know. OK, I'll find out.'

'No hurry, love. Idle curiosity.'

Mike's speech

For the second year running, Mike sat on the platform at the United Peace Movement's Annual General Meeting, a member of the Executive Committee. This year they didn't re-elect him. No wonder. The liberals didn't like the way he pushed illegal action. The Reds thought he was a Trot, the Trots thought he was an anarchist, the anarchists thought he was a Red. They were all correct. They were attacking Mike for not being a politician, which he wasn't, however hard he tried. But soon after the ballot and the big wind-up speeches, the conference began to turn into a reunion dance, the bar opened and the delegates began to cluster in corners, adding up gains and losses. Mike, who was due to speak at a fringe meeting directly after the conference, bought half a bottle of brandy, made for Room 18 and waited for eight o'clock, when he was due to speak. His speech was to be called 'The Same Old Problems'. He hadn't written it. He had started seven times, but it never worked.

At 8.15 there were ten people sitting around the room, most of them at least three rows away. Mike swigged at the brandy. About quarter of the bottle was left. He stood up, walked the width of the room three times and then again:

'Love is more complicated than chess, and chess is something that nobody knows completely. Children often cry because the world is hard to bear. Men cry only when their armour (or their skin) is ripped off them, leaving their softness. Children cry. Women cry. And men cry. It is important to cry, to be able to cry.

'So, this softness. These are my hands, all right? Two hands, one calloused with work and weather, one pampered by air-conditioning and soap. Our hands, I mean. The calloused hand can be used to shift weights, sacks or pianos, but it can't respond in all that exquisite detail to textures. It can vote to strike. But the soft hand, well, it's sensitive, useless in most sorts of positive action, except making love. We can't afford refinement, exquisite bloody textures. Hunger, poverty, war say we can't. There's not enough time to play about with our sensitivities. England's cluttered, smothered, jammed up to the gums with charming irrelevancies. Choking.

'Love changes from second to second, just as the body's chemistry changes. Suddenly, sometimes, it comes into my whole brain and body without warning. Just trying to tell you the truth about a few things, the few things I know about. It's like, suddenly, all my blood's been drained out and replaced with liquid gold or silver or brandy, that's the most likely. What would the working classes do with more leisure? Eat, drink and fuck, I hope.

'Asia is a huge animal. Always its body shouts with hunger or pain. Sometimes one of its limbs winces, flails, contracts or jerks with a special, local pain. This animal is more interesting than we are.

'If wishes were horses we'd all be stamped to death from inside. I know damn well the nothing chances of ever living to breathe on a basically non-violent, co-operative, free planet, which is not of course all I want, but simply what I need before I can begin to go happily about my business and desires, for every man has business and desires. My business, my real business, my secret business is dancing. Nobody's ever guessed yet, or caught me at it, it's not in my palm, my birthsign or my passport. I never took a dancing class, wow, they cripple you with their mince-around pirouette up your own tutu, you know, these European dancers on porcelain legs. Not that. The Russians are a bit more like it. Some of the African tribes are nearer still to the kind of dancing I want, the kind for which you have to start off happy and get happier. And you have to dance naked. And you need the whole globe.

'I want too much. I want peace. Want socialism. Want freedom. I want the godblasted Dark Ages to come to an end.

'I met the owner of a firm which builds estates when I was covering a dinner for a newspaper. He said: "There's a good deal of solid wealth down here in the West Country. There are several millionaires here tonight. But they're very gracious, human. Sir Bum Bum, he's a very rich man, he was down by the harbour in old yachting clothes and a man came up, from the North, and asked – I can't do the accent – 'Where can I hire a boat?' And you know, Sir Bum Bum explained very carefully. And the man tipped him sixpence. Now you know, he didn't stand on his dignity. And Sir Harold Harold over there, he's here, just talking to everyone, no reason why he shouldn't, of course. And you know, if they were in Russia, they'd be put up against a wall and shot." The way he described it you could almost see the bullet-holes.

'The odds are fiercely against us. There's very little hope. Which is why so many people who used to work in the Peace Movement come to me with a half-smile and say, hasn't the movement had it? Isn't it all over? Can't we all go home or lie back and enjoy it, we'll never get rid of the bomb any more than a hunchback loses his hump, and after all it never dropped in Cuba Week. I can hardly talk back at them any more, my throat gets all clogged up with sticky blackness because of course I've felt all that despair, of course I know about that, but I won't bloody use it, simply because it's useless. The odds. Hey, count the odds. They may be ninety-nine to one against us or worse. But I only care about that sweet one per cent. All my life there have been wars going on, Probably the rest of my life will be spent in wartime. Tough titty. I'm only interested in how much peace and socialism and freedom can be grabbed, grabbed because you know damn well they've never given us anything worth having. That one-per-cent hope is about the only interesting thing in the world. If you don't struggle, you're not alive, yes that's a slogan but slogans can work. If King Kong's blundering along down Fifth Avenue holding a blonde in his fist and she's not moving you say, well either she must like it or she's dead – either way there's no reason to stop and help her. No struggle, no survival. Obvious. Eight of you left, that's fine. I may walk out on myself for that matter. But maybe one of you will feel it, that the big risks are the only ones worth taking and if we get that sweet one per cent we'll not be satisfied, contented, because to be contented is to die. Yes. No end to this struggle stuff. No sudden breakthrough, no going up to a mountain top, gaping in wonder and then galloping down to the promised land. Nothing like that, nothing like peace of bloody mind. There's never been a victory day which didn't stink of gangrene. No ending. If some politician announces that his state has reached socialist perfection, all you can do is pity his little pointed head. Because he's found a cage he likes, he reckons everyone else loves life in the zoo. So treat him as you'd treat a fellow-prisoner who's chatty with the warders.

'Measure every civilization by the way it treats its enemies, its poor and its prisoners. The House of Commons is Washington's dolls' house. Buckingham Palace is only semi-detached from Wormwood Scrubs.

'I spent last weekend with friends in deep suburbia. Among all the black-beamed and roomy new houses, the children visit each other by appointment. There are many children, all of them in bright clothes. When a father leaves his house in his washed car, his children flutter round the doors calling their goodbyes. It looks like a safe place. There is even a beauty about it. It looks so safe.

'I want to talk to you for ever. I won't. I love you. No, I don't, I don't know you, there's a half-light in here through which I can hardly see you. But your faces shine, or something behind your faces shines. The truth, the truth is, I want to love you. But we're afraid of each other. You're afraid of me, shovelling my guts out like a stoker, croaking out of the top of my brandy brain, refusing to stop, letting it all pour out, afraid to stop because to stop might mean I would have to be silent for ever. Trying to be honest. Please take it and use it if you can. Maybe what I see has nothing to do with your version of this planet. That's partly why I'm afraid of you. We can hurt each other in a thousand ways.

'I was on a bus sitting behind a mother showing her son the sights of London. He said: "Will C & A's take over Marks & Spencer's?" She said: "No, they are far too well established."

'I'm trying to teach myself to be free. That means trying to erase all the lessons I've been taught by social and economic punishments and rewards, it means diving straight down towards what seems to be true water, keeping my eyes open as I dive. When it works, I love the dive. When I smash on the concrete, I forget it.

'I suppose you know everything I know.

'Asia is not an animal. Asia is the name of this slim girl, her eyes like islands, who moves like silk. As she moves, the air moves like silk. Full-coloured fruit crowds the barrows in the market-place, but as she raises this orange to her lips, the air is suddenly full of three-foot truncheons, semicircular steel helmets, black truncheons and one leather-gloved hand at the back of her throat and one truncheon across the straight parting of her night-coloured hair and the truncheon falls and the camera moves to someone in the English studio who thinks that was bad with someone who thinks that was good. And there's an impartial chairman.

'Why work? Take an example. You're in a bathroom. You take a slimy old face-flannel and flip and rub and squeeze and dip and rub again until the grime is all washed away from the white paintwork of the bathroom window-frame. Why do that? So that the paint will reflect the light more clearly, so there will be more light for your eyes to enjoy? Or maybe you're doing it for someone else? Who's in your mind as you squint down to make sure the interstices of that window-frame are free from grit? Someone you love, who'll take pleasure in that extra, bouncing light? Or someone you fear? Someone who employs you, who'll become more terrifying with every scrap of dirt you leave behind? And whose bathroom is it? Do you rent it, or own it? Are you even allowed to take a bath in it yourself?

'I think I was dropped from Mars. No, we know too much about Mars. I think I was dropped from some planet which hasn't got a name. I say I was dropped because I can't imagine myself volunteering for the jump. I'm not adventurous. Lack courage. Bruise easily. I think I speak for us all, all us aliens. This is the odd thing, or rather one of the odd things in a world which itself looks and feels and smells like an oddity to me. I feel like an alien, but I have the idea that there are other aliens.

'I will start again. I hear a car's brake cry out. I can hear the impatience inside you. I can also hear your hunger. I can smell your love, whoever it may be for. My trousers are itching slightly, I don't like them. I am very tired. Help me. Thank you.

'Maybe that was a joke. I would tell you a joke, but everything seems funny one moment and the next moment nothing seems funny.

'I will start again. I am interested in complete activity and complete peace. Total. I believe in talking totally, writing totally, watching and listening totally, making love totally, reading totally and, as often as possible, sleeping totally.

'I know I'm absurd. I don't mind. All the people I love are absurd. But I can say anything I like. No, I can't, but I can say more than I ever could before.

'Asia is a revolver.

'With one hand I'm trying to grab all the freedom I can grab. Thought, movement, speech, love – the whole bloody lot. Never mind what I'm doing with the other.

'Asia is the brain of a man who is being given, with the consent of his close relatives, electric-shock treatment.'

Mike had to stop there, he was too tired. There were only five people left. One of them, a girl with extremely large eyes, followed him to the bar. The inside of his head now felt jagged and white, polar. He had wept at least three tears as he had spoken and failed to speak. Now a thousand tears threatened. The girl gave him a whisky and smiled. Afraid to thank her for the whisky, her eyes or the smile she gave him, he perched on the end of a trestle table and sucked the edge of his tumbler. I've just spoken, he thought, as well as I could, spoken terribly, now let me rest, let me for blood's sake get some rest, stop nagging, my brain's racing, put on the brake, brake the damn thing, brake.

He gulped whisky. It burned. Make me glow, make me sick, make me glow. Peace. Oil my grating brain-wheels. Peace. His brain, surprised by the change from brandy to whisky, tried to hold up a placard reading 'Peace Can Only Be Attained by the Concerted Action of the Peoples of the World on Socialist Lines' – but Mike said to his brain quietly: I know. His brain let the heavy placard drop.

Mike turned to the girl. Her lips were heavy, her hips were heavy. As she flushed he knew that he was certainly in love with her, for giving him so much comfort when he needed nothing else. For being quietly with him. She was about fifteen.

She said, after they'd been talking for a few minutes:

'It's not really speeches or anything that made me march and go to meetings. It's the girls at school. You know what they're like, most of them wouldn't admit it, but we all want to have children some day. All of us. And American girls and Russian girls and Chinese must be the same. So you have to do something, don't you? We just don't want anyone killing our babies.'

She stopped and her face reddened. She'd noticed that Mike was crying.

'I'm sorry,' he said.

'That's all right,' she said. 'I'm just not sure what to do to help you. How drunk are you?'

'I'm a bit gone. Look, I wish ... Look, I've got to get home and get some sleep. But I'd better tell you that I love you for what you are, and for being with me and for saying what you said.'

'I love you,' she said. 'Well, I love quite a lot of people, but you're included now. I'm not after you or anything, but I love you.'

'Among others.'

'Well, that's right, isn't it?'

'That's right.'

He kissed her and then he went back to his attic alone.

Report on campaign by Lorna

A. *The Destruction of Rodney*

Rodney believes deeply in his own niceness. He believes that gentlemen are gentlemen until proved otherwise. He once had vaguely liberal ideals. These were easily burnt out without him feeling any pain. His career, which I followed and in part directed, went as follows.

Oxford. Worked hard for a good degree in languages, French and German. Took some part in politics (Liberal Club), but was weaned away from politics, partly by a series of escalating revelations about political corruption, partly by my appearance on the scene as a muse, encouraging him to write his little poems. Rodney went down from Oxford to the job I had prepared for him on the literary magazine *British Letters.*

British Letters. BL was of course a CIA-financed operation. Rodney did not know this. He was satisfactory as a poem-sorter and developed a kind of wit and some popularity at publishers' parties. He brought out his first volume of poems. After two years, Tom Wilkinson left Rodney in charge of *BL* while he went on a four-month sabbatical to the USA. At this point I encouraged Rodney to ask Mike for a contribution. Mike submitted, as I'd hoped, a 10,000-word diatribe against Washington's policy in Latin America. Rodney fell for the article, which was well written and documented, saying that it would 'give balance' to *BL.* Wilkinson returned to find the article set up in proof, and advised Rodney to find another job, as Mike's article was 'hopelessly old-fashioned'.

Multicolor Advertising. I was on hand to comfort Rodney, and after three weeks in Mallorca I had him grovelling for marriage. I married him and he took the job I found for him as a copy-writer with Multicolor. His small poems became smaller. Despite some qualms, he was promoted from a stocking to a cigarette account. At weekends we entertained a series of economists, journalists and history dons at the Hall. They were helpful in making Rodney politically sensible.

Global Image. This is a large organization with offices in every Western capital, paying high salaries and employing the best double-checked men at often boring jobs. Rodney was put to work on what is known as the German account. His job, broadly, was and is to check British newspapers, magazines and books for references to twentieth-century Germany. The aim is threefold: to modify the image of Nazi Germany, to improve the image of Western Germany and to corrode the image of Eastern Germany (if that's possible). Action, which includes initiating letters to the Press, the appearance of experts on television, specially written articles, etc., is never identifiable as the work of Global Image.

Future. Rodney's initiation into Global Image was gently and gradually done. As he begins to face the implications of his work, and he has already discovered facts which would disturb most men, his nerves will become more brittle. Already he is drinking heavily. This will be encouraged. He may drink himself to death. Or he may crash his car while drunk. I don't think he has more than a couple of years to go now. In the meantime, he is useful.

B. *The Destruction of Jack*

Jack's imagination is about all he ever had. When I met him it was directed towards other people. I had to turn it inwards. After they let him out of hospital I took him in at the Hall and became his mistress. My whole policy with Jack has been based on the old principle of alternating kindness with brutality as unpredictably and variously as possible. (This has also been my sexual policy with Rodney since our marriage.) I used drugs, combined with his terror of the bomb, to drive him mad and keep him mad. I used good and bad sex to keep him under control. His friendship with Mike seemed the only danger. I slandered Mike deliberately until Jack was sick of the name. About a year ago, I told Jack that Mike had killed himself. That also helped the madness. Rodney, who has never fully understood my relationship with Jack, has co-operated in his treatment in every way.

C. *The Destruction of Mike*

This one, Father, has gone wrong. Mike's own aim appeared to be to become a leftist politician or a journalist. My aim was to help him to start in this direction and then to cut him down. But after I had him sacked from the *Gazette*, he became elusive. I hired a private detective who has filled several ledgers and files with notes, documents, tape-recordings and photographs which could destroy the career or family of any ordinary man. But Mike has no career and no family. He operates alone, mimeographing his own bloody red broadsheet. He can't even be thrown out of a party, because he doesn't belong to one. He can't be prosecuted satisfactorily, because when he breaks the law, he does it publicly. I've tried to get some good 'peace movement' rumours circulating – Mike's CIA, that sort of thing – but they haven't worked with most people. Now the other two are almost finished, I must concentrate on Mike. I may have to kill him. I wouldn't mind killing him at all. If it happened at the Hall it could be self-defence, I'm sure Rodney would agree after the event. (Jack wouldn't look too well on the witness stand.) Anyway, Rodney can write to Mike and tell him that Jack now lives at the Hall, is very ill and wants to see him urgently. And Mike will come. And then I'll see what has to be done.

End
1963

December 5th, 1963, began, a strange day like all other days, adding up
WATER DOCTOR ASSAULTED RELIGIOUS EQUIPMENT
like all other days. Two miners were drowned at Saarbrucken, West Germany,
ELDERLY HARVEST BURNED
when water broke into a working of the Maybach pit. President
BLANKET JUDGE DISMISSED
Kasavubu of the Congo began his state visit to Israel and Madame Nhu
WINE GUERRILLAS SPOOF LITERATURE LEADER
arrived in Paris to write her memoirs. Statistics released in Moscow
MINERS GIVEN BOMB CARTS
showed that the harvest in the steppes of Central Asia had been a disaster.
POLICE UNDRESS
Governor John Conally of Texas, wounded when President Kennedy was
GOSPEL DOCTOR LAUNCHED
assassinated, was released from hospital. In Graz, Austria, three
BALL CAMPAIGN PLOTTED
children were burned to death by an electric blanket. In Ankara, Turkey,
DEATH ACCUSED
death sentences were reaffirmed on three men charged with taking part
JUMPING TEETH INFLUENCED MILITARY STATUS
in the May 21st revolt. There was a threat to British property in
PROPERTY PIT HOLDING ELECTRIC WEAPONS
Caracas, Mr Winston Field of Southern Rhodesia attacked Britain for
MURDER PRESIDENT BEAMS
withholding his country's independence, and vinegrowers in the

Department
PAIN MEADOW INVITATION TO SKY WITNESS
of Herault, France, blocked at least seven roads with barricades of
RACIAL ROCKET ANNOUNCED
beams, posts, carts, old tyres and stones in protest against imported
BANNED CHILDREN COMMITTING SILENCE
cheap red wine.
PRISON LOVER IDENTIFIED AND BLOCKED

At the sabotage trial in Pretoria, Walter Sisulu, Nelson Mandela and
FOREMAN KICKED TRUTH
eight others were in the dock. A prosecution witness, Thomas Mashifane, who
CHEAP REPORTERS HOLDING HIGHLIGHT
was foreman of the labourers at the farm where the accused had allegedly
INDECENT COALITION ACCEPTED WORLD-FAMOUS LOVER
plotted, said that when his statement had been taken by the police, they
DROWNED OFFICE CONVENTION FOUNDED
told him it had not been given properly. He said they told him to undress
ALL-TIME PERSON FARM IDENTIFIED
and run around a table. As he did so, they kicked and hit him. He said
MASS HISTORY REVEALED BY MILITARY VINEGROWERS
he still suffered from the effects of blows on his right ear and one of
SUICIDE CONVENTION AT ATOMIC UNIVERSITY
his teeth was loose. 'I just wanted to know why I should be assaulted
INDUSTRIAL CAPTORS HIT EXCELLENT MAN
like that when I was not committing any offence,' he said. The prosecutor,
STONES DOCTOR ALLEGEDLY GIVEN TABLE
Dr Percy Yutar, said the accusation came as a complete surprise; he had

SPOOF LOVER BURNED MURDER PIT
asked the witness if he had any complaints and Mashifane has said not.
BOMB WATER BEAMS SKY
Asked by the judge if his treatment had influenced his statement, Mashifane
BLANKET DROWNED
said he had told the truth: 'But certain things I said, I did not say as
ELDERLY BALL BLOCKED BY RELIGIOUS ROCKET
I would have wanted to say on my own. I want to explain it in this way: when
PAIN REPORTERS FOUNDED TRUTH CARTS
a person is being kicked, then he cannot speak as he would have wanted to
WORLD-FAMOUS SUICIDE BEAMS BANNED
speak if he had not been suffering pain.' Later in the day, Dr Yutar
PROPERTY COALITION GUERRILLAS UNDRESS DROWNED CHILDREN
said to the judge that there had been an immediate investigation of
WINE UNIVERSITY INFLUENCED MINERS
Mashifane's charges. Witness had declined to make a statement and had begged
BOMB COALITION HOLDING BURNED CHILDREN
him not to take the matter any further. An appeal by Sisulu against a
ELECTRIC JUDGE ASSAULTED ALL-TIME TEETH
six-year jail sentence for allegedly holding office in the banned African
WEAPONS DOCTOR IDENTIFIED INDECENT HIGHLIGHT
National Congress and an appeal by Mrs Helen Joseph against a one-year
VINEGROWERS HOLDING SKY FOREMAN
suspended sentence for failing on one occasion to report to the police
ATOMIC COALITION UNDRESS SOCIALIST STONES
were dismissed by the Pretoria Supreme Court.
CHILDREN CARTS HIT DEATH HARVEST

A new socialist coalition took office in Italy. A religious group of
BALL OFFICE INVITATION TO MINERS
76 people left Brownsville, Texas, to live in the back-country of Paraguay
EXCELLENT GOSPEL BOMB INFLUENCED PAIN POLICE
and preach the gospel. Mr Henrik Beer, Swedish Secretary-General of the
LOVER HOLDING SKY BURNED WATER
League of Red Cross Societies said in Geneva that the Chinese were launching
BURNED WATER KICKED INDUSTRIAL HISTORY
a big birth-control campaign. Herbert Lehman, who supported FDR, fought
INDUSTRIAL HISTORY BLOCKED BY PRISON GUERRILLAS
against MacCarthyism and racial discrimination, died at 85 in New York.
GUERRILLAS ALLEGEDLY UNDRESS TABLE HIGHLIGHT
Mr Hussein Shaheed Suhrawardy, former Prime Minister of Pakistan, died
HIGHLIGHT ALL-TIME WORLD-FAMOUS EXCELLENT BLANKET
in Beirut at 70.
BLANKET INVITATION TO SPOOF PAIN WEAPONS LAUNCHED

It was a Thursday. In Venezuela, Red guerrillas freed US Colonel
STONES INFLUENCED TEETH
James K. Chenault at dawn. Chenault told reporters that his captors tried
WORLD-FAMOUS BOMB FARM GIVES SPOOF FOREMAN
brainwashing him, but that he responded with some facts about American
WINE BEAMS
life – 'The status of the military in the United States, our laws, our
SPOOF MEADOW ANNOUNCED
police system and family life.' He said: 'I don't know if they were interested
SUICIDE MILLIONAIRE HOLDING HARVEST CHILDREN
but they listened.'

TRUTH MURDER BY PROPERTY ROCKET

A Hamburg rocket firm revealed that it had tested rockets in

ELDERLY REPORTERS BURNED HIGHLIGHT CARTS

foreign countries in order to get round Brussels Treaty restrictions on

ELDERLY CHILDREN REVEALED ALL-TIME BOMB MILLIONAIRE

West Germany. It planned to test military rockets in West Germany

VINEGROWERS UNDRESS ELECTRIC FOREMAN

during 1964. The firm announced this at a demonstration of four

EXCELLENT MURDER OFFICE BURNED

'scientific' rockets launched from a meadow near Cuxhaven. There were about

UNIVERSITY MINERS SPOOF ELECTRIC SKY

20 guests at the demonstration, but the head of the firm, the Weapons and

WINE ROCKET JUMPING

Aviation Equipment Company, said they did not want to be identified. Two

INDECENT BLANKET CONVENTION BY ATOMIC CHILDREN

of the guests were military attachés at the Jordanian and Saudi Arabian

ALL-TIME ELECTRIC PRISON STATUS HIT

Embassies in Bonn.

SILENCE BY WATER

A spoof on world-famous millionaires was the highlight of the

INDECENT TRUTH BOMB HIT BY RACIAL HARVEST

Millionaires' Ball in Chicago. An elderly man became the 328th person to

ELECTRIC MURDER CARTS BANNED

commit suicide by jumping off the Eiffel Tower. The Ministry of Justice in

SKY HISTORY GROWERS INVITATION TO JUMPING BALL CHILDREN

Kiel announced the arrest of Werner Meyer, chief police commissioner of the

EXCELLENT RELIGIOUS PIT HOLDING ELECTRIC GUERRILLAS

Schleswig-Holstein CID, on charges of being involved in the mass murder

INDUSTRIAL PAIN PRESIDENT INFLUENCED BY WINE BLANKET
of Jews. He was an SS Obersturmführer and leader of a command of the state
HISTORY ASSAULTED BY ELECTRIC LOVER BEAMS
security police in Russia in 1943. An East–West conference in Moscow opened
TRUTH MILLIONAIRE HIT BY SKY
with a minute's silence for the late President Kennedy and Pope John. Dr
LITERATURE GUERRILLAS HOLDING ELDERLY BLANKET
Ralph Lapp, a physicist who worked on the atomic bomb, said in Charlotte,
INDECENT JUDGE HOLDING WORLD-FAMOUS LOVER STONES
North Carolina, that American 'spy in the sky' satellites were providing
BALL CARTS BURNED BY PAIN GROWERS
excellent photographs of Russian military installations. In Capetown a
CHEAP TRUTH IDENTIFIED AT BOMB UNIVERSITY
former university lecturer had her sentence of a year in prison for talking
HIGHLIGHT FARM BLOCKED BY CHEAP MURDER STATUS
to her politically banned lover cut to one month. President Lyndon Johnson
BOMB TABLE DROWNED BY SILENCE
lunched with Senator Harry F. Byrd, received from Representative Fred
MINERS CLIMB ELECTRIC BARRICADES THREAT TO BRITISH SPOOF WHITE PAIN
Schwengel the first copy of a new history of the Capitol, received
PROPERTY WOUNDED CHEAP PAIN SPREADERS PRESENTATION HOLDING ELECTRIC PIT
an invitation from the American Legion to speak at its annual convention
MURDER SATELLITE PRESENTATION PROPERTY BRAINWASH ROCKET JUMPING
in Dallas, accepted the resignation of the ambassador to the Congo
ANOTHER MOSCOW TO DIE ANOTHER CHICAGO ANOTHER

BONN ANOTHER
and met separately with the President of the Brotherhood of Sleeping
GOSPEL JAIL MOURNS ELECTRIC NAZI COALITION SUICIDE SKY
Car Porters, the Chairman of the Joint Chiefs of Staff, the secretary
BAD SPOOF PILL FOR BRUTALITY PRESIDENT ELECTRIC HARVEST BARRICADES
of Welfare and the National Security Council. Hugh Hefner, publisher of
SLEEPING NAZI BOMB ASSAULTED BRAINWASH BROTHERHOOD WATER
Playboy magazine, charged with selling obscene literature, said in Chicago
UNDRESS RACIAL UNDRESS SPY UNDRESS BOMB UNDRESS SATELLITE UNDRESS UNDRESS
that each person should be his own judge of what is acceptable. In Jersey
UNDRESS UNIVERSITY UNDRESS PAIN UNDRESS PROPERTY UNDRESS JUDGE UNDRESS
the headmaster of a preparatory school was jailed for six years for
UNDRESS COALITION UNDRESS HARVEST CHILDREN UNDRESS RELIGIOUS UNDRESS
indecent assaults against three boarders. On Wall Street the Dow
UNDRESS ATOMIC UNDRESS PRESIDENT UNDRESS PRISON UNDRESS DOCTOR UNDRESS
Jones industrial share index closed at a new all-time peak with
UNDRESS REPORTERS UNDRESS TRUTH UNDRESS ATOMIC OFFICE UNDRESS LOVER
a rise of 8·35 to 763·86.

Quite apart from this, which all adds up and much more easily now than it did then, the English newspapers illuminated other corners. The *Daily Mirror* showed scenes from the 'screen's most amazing bedroom scene' and columnist Marjorie Proops asked, 'What's wrong with love in the afternoon, Vicar?' Five editorials in the *Daily Express*. 'How sensible of Pope Paul to decide to visit the Holy Land.' 'Plainly foreigners must treat our trawlers better or we must treat theirs worse.' 'The decision to get rid of the Woolwich Arsenal is a wise one.' 'The mixed-manned Polaris fleet is rejected by the countries of the Western European Union.' 'Stories of rapacious landlords, of disputes between tenants and landlords, often make the headlines. Yet in the overwhelming number of cases, the relationship is a happy one. For many tenants the landlord is also a friend.' The *Daily Mail* discussed the effect of President Kennedy's assassination on the South. In the *Daily Worker*, Barbara Niven thanked readers for beating the paper's £3,750 target in honour of its ten-thousandth issue.

In most of the papers the critics were talking about the arts as if they owned them:

No doubt it cheers someone to think of his money being spent by the Arts Council to keep bead-making and free verse alive in the little marshland villages and scattered hamlets of provincial Britain. There is no plot. Everybody appears to be wading through glue both mentally and physically. Every image is perfect but bears little relationship to the one following. His own best poems are like simple, evocative images etched with stone on stone. With the aid of spare but highly evocative piano figuration. From then on the play descends in swiftly moving circles of pain, anguish and despair which are only tolerable if they strike answering chords of pity and awe.

He writes easily in a style that is more accurately described as pointilliste than impressionist, glittering when it comes off but sometimes only a collection of gaily coloured unrelated spots. But there is an opposite side to the coin. But displayed an admirable dramatic sense and immense rhythmic brio. But, as it were, in a hypnotic state. But the total gesture was, strangely enough, rather muffled. But for the most part the longer pieces do not keep up the finesse of their openings. Moving, but not perfect. Finally, a verse play, two anthologies and an encyclopaedia.

It was the birthday of Sir Edgar Cohen, 55; Mr William Devlin, 52; Miss Enid M. Essame, 57; Major-General H. R. B. Foote, VC, 59; Professor C. F. Powell, 60; Dame Mary Smieton, 61; Sir Reader Bulliard, 78; The Earl of Longford, 58; Lord Rotherwick, 51; Lord Nathan, 41; and Lord Napier and Ettrick, 33. It was also the thirtieth anniversary of the repeal of prohibition in the United States, and the engagement of the Hon C. W.

Joynson-Hicks to Miss G. E. Schulter was announced.

In the advertisement columns of the *Daily Telegraph*, St Luke's Nursing Home for the Clergy asked for subscriptions, donations and legacies; Well-Known Author asked for postal pupils; The Lincoln Cathedral Appeal, The Cathedral, Lincoln (threatened with partial collapse, repairs have begun to the roof-timbers ravaged by death-watch beetles and dangerous stone-work), asked for another £100,000; Brookland Hill School, Welshpool, said that while it did not guarantee success in the Common Entrance or the GCE, in the event of failure boys would be prepared again free of all fees.

Salesmen were wanted to sell exclusive knitwear, cartons, industrial cranes, Nationally Advertised Products (I. B. Kleinwort Rubber Co), illuminated and suspended ceilings, metal windows, cosmetics and portable buildings. Harwell's Irradiation Branch wanted Physicists and Metallurgists with interests in the Solid State field. The Chair of Preventative Dentistry at Edinburgh University was also advertised. The University of Aberdeen needed a Lecturer in the Department of Biblical Criticism. Nineteen births, one marriage and thirty-four deaths were announced on page one of *The Times*, which also advertised two important jobs in the flavour industry and positions in a Chinese restaurant in Oslo for a 'sober first-class Chinese cook (chef) and two assistant cooks ... Good salary and treatment'.

There was a wide choice of cars in the £4,000–£5,000 price range offered in *The Times* and several for under £1,000. High-class flats and maisonettes in Hans Place on forty-year leases were offered from £13,500 to £32,500. A good-class manservant was required for a temporary post in a Gentleman's Country House and a Chauffeur with Rolls experience was needed in Eaton Square. In the personal columns, Frances, Countess Lloyd George of Dwyfor, explained that she was sending money to the Church Overseas instead of Christmas cards, at the request of the Bishop of Guildford. One stall for the Fonteyn–Nureyev *Swan Lake* was offered in exchange for one Callas *Tosca*. The Home of Rest for Horses, Boreham Wood, asked for donations. Young bachelor, ex-Scout, sought congenial responsible male to share London flat. Own Room. The Society for the Assistance of Ladies in Reduced Circumstances asked for donations and Miss Ollivier advertised Colonic Irrigation. Stimulating.

December 5th, 1963. It was a long drive. Mike armoured himself in black leather and crash helmet, slipped his goggles down and made the bike roar. The labour-movement puritan in Mike's head immediately sneered, pointing out that he was wearing the uniform and mask of an alienated delinquent. The anarchist in the other side of his head argued that England needed bigger and better alienated delinquents. Subversion, that's the song. Mike shook his haggling head. He had to get from London to Belston and then out to the Hall and he couldn't afford a car or a train. Leather was the best protection on the market. It didn't matter what he looked like, he wasn't representing any organization, not any more, he wasn't trying to impress anyone, not any more.

Very early in the journey, about the moment he passed a sign saying Laughing Dog Food, he remembered that he wanted a woman badly. Well, he wanted a woman well. It should be ideal, it should leave them both feeling fuller and freer – Mike tried to erase this sidetracking idea by contemplating food, not dog food but Mike food, massed eggs with beans and chips, but the technicolour plateful kept cooling and congealing in his mind and he looked up from the imaginary table into a pair of naked feminine eyes. He tried thinking about Lyndon Johnson, but a woman kept swaying back into his brain, a woman shape which kept changing shape. He couldn't see her face. Realizing that he might as well surrender to his groiny daydreams, he opened his eyes wider than usual, locked them to the road ahead and let the woman, the women, sway around his mind as they would, play with him as they wished. Legends about knights distracted from their quests by shining bodies became meaningless.

He sped mentally through old and new scenes: at first he tried to make them socially realistic – he would cruise into a lorrydrivers' cafe and find her. As he munched into the double egg, chips and beans, rich with grease and chemically complex sauce, he would notice a girl with smudged white trousers standing in front of the jukebox, one hand on either flank of the box, absorbing the vibrations as she played, over and over again, the same rhythm-and-blues number. A few lorrydrivers were laughing at her arse, which could not quite stay still. She didn't seem afraid of them but she didn't fancy them enough to ask for a lift. Then she turned and saw Mike. The lorrydrivers flew out of focus, their laughter was wiped from the soundtrack. Her long hair sparkled in a hundred places – no, kill that, that image jumped out of the shampoo commercials. Her long hair did not sparkle with cartoon stars, but it seemed clean, she had been swimming in some river, some clean river. What clean river? The hell with geography. Her long hair looked all right. It was clean. She had washed it, just because she had a beat look about her eyes didn't mean she didn't wash her hair. It even sparkled a bit. Why should her hair matter? It mattered. She was a neat beat. Her suede jacket for instance, it wasn't even torn or worn to a shine. Enough of sartorial details, what did she look like? Beautiful. No, that's much too vague, that gives me no tug at all. Long green eyes. Long green eyes. Good. A wet, rolled-over lower lip. Wet? She'd been licking it. Hips slim enough and mobile with music. Breasts? Well, what do you want, firm, small and high or firm, full and deep? Not sure. Medium deep, all right? Identity? Unknown, unimportant. She sat down and picked a chip off his plate, a fat chip, looking up immediately for a reaction before biting its end off. She wore a CND badge, a good signal. Was she black? No, save that for the next dream. OK. She sighed. 'Wish life was simple,' she said. 'Why?' 'Then I could say to you, I fancy you like mad, give us a lift five miles up the road to my pad. Got a lot of vodka there from somewhere.' From nowhere she produced a prop which Mike forgot to include earlier in the scene, a fat joint, lit it, puffed and passed it over. Mike inhaled and his heart jumped. 'Life's simple enough. I fancy you too,' he said. 'Let's go to Fanny Hill Land.' Her whole face transmitted gratitude for the gift of Mike, she wriggled as she said: 'You're beautiful.' 'You're beautiful,' he said back, and out they walked together into the sunset, no it was dark. Naturally, as they rode, he could feel her heated nipples pressing through the back of his jacket. The electrodes of her nipples or some such red-in-the-face phrase. Mike's imagination was tripping over itself as the mental travellers neared the girl's place. He hadn't even given the girl a name yet. He immediately named her Rosa, a good name for whispering, a name that glowed in the dark.

He decided that, for added interest, she lived on an island in a river which ran through a wood, an island reached by a leaking white boat with short, cracked oars. On the island – a wooden house, long and low, tumbling slightly, stacked with paintings, good paintings but not too good. (If he made her a genius she might forget him in the urge to gouache. So good paintings, not great ones, splurged all over with passionate colours. Good.) It was one big, ramshackle room with a brass bedstead at the end, it was warm although Mike couldn't decide how it was heated. A stove would be too much trouble, hopping out of bed twice a night to stoke, and electricity, on the island, seemed unrealistic. But the thick fur of the rugs was unrealistic too, so were the bottles and the bucket of ice which materialized from the thin air of his imagination. She moved so quickly. In one motion she had put on a noisy Chuck Berry LP, poured them both drinks, peeled her jacket and begun to dance at him, had fallen over backwards on the rug, was laughing, talking, silent, hugging his head all at the same time. Too quick. He went back in time. From a bookcase, a white bookcase, she took an LP by an American vocal group he'd never heard about. The record sleeve was extraordinary because its shapes and colours shifted as he stared at them, just as her shapes and colours seemed to shift (see any textbook or happy article about the effects of drugs). With a smiling shrug, a shrugging smile he unzipped his black jacket, draping it over a hook which appeared just before his fingers let go of the jacket. To take stock, he was now wearing a T-shirt, leather trousers, Y-fronts, socks, heavy shoes. The record wailed, jerky solid noises. She said something nice about his arms, but what did she say? 'You have nice arms.' No, that was a nothing, Surbiton statement. 'Brown fur on brown arms,' that was more like it, sounded like some sort of painter. Now? No, wait, make it last. Drinks. She poured them each a vodka, a lot of vodka, Russian stuff, into two jam jars made of thick, distorting glass. Into each jar she dropped ice and sprinkled it with some scarlet juice from a small bottle with a close-printed label, not fruit juice or tomato juice, something strange.

Strange? Uncanny – yes – a comic-book, science-fiction cocktail whose side-effects included the repealing of the law of gravity, the melting of all clothing, the withering away of all the inhibitions, the granting of the gift of tongues, a crown of flames, the doubling of virility after the first time, quadrupling after the second time and so on, upwards and onwards. No. No good, too vague, too vague. Mike emptied the drinks down the sink and they each sank a straight vodka, sitting opposite each other on the floor, cross-legged, meditating on each other's bodies. They crawled together and began to undress each other. Good, realistically erotic without departing from the principles of sexual equality. Although this night-time daydreaming was a departure from other principles, probably. Did Lenin, in his prison, using bread inkwells and writing his proclamations in milk while his Krupskaya stood on the pavement outside hoping that he might see her, need sexual fantasies? Maybe not, but Mike knew damn well he was less than Lenin. They were naked now and she was slippery with olive oil, for Christ's sake where did she get that stuff, and now they were, as they rolled, slid and collided softly, both lubricated totally with the oil. Now, how do you do? Very well, thank you. Yes, but how do you want to? Any way. Mike tried it on the floor but there was a draught, in the bath but the water began to cool, across the bed, in the bed – that was best, even if he couldn't imagine it with absolutely clean sheets and the blankets were brown and frayed. Could she have perfume as well as olive oil? Why not? All right, one green-eyed bird in oil with perfume coming up. Up, up and away with Superman Mike. That's how it would be. And away and away. Afterwards an extraordinary meal including chicken and wine, then more of the same but different. Finally the grown-up farewell as he mounts his bike and waves a heavy glove. He'll always be welcome but he'll never have to return. And of course she has a flat in Belston too, she'll always be loving and lovely and handy and never ask too much.

Mike began to laugh at himself, at his Bohemian Ideal Home, at the kind of romanticism which made fetishes of chicken, long hair, rowdy pop records and the CND badge. As he leaned into the turn from the dual carriageway into the Belston road he remembered that the beat girl dream had begun as a realistic exercise. But why had it started at all? I haven't had it off for a week, he thought. That's the unholy, unhealthy truth. A tune which was mainly rhythm began to beat in his head and chanted. 'My name is Mike. I've got a tool like a microphone tonight.' He shouted against the wind, against the vibrato of his engine. 'Come on then, you big dreamer. Hey baldy, loud-mouthed, blind philosopher. You stark old rod, pretentious log, think straight.' It became a formless ballad, the tune changing with every line.

'Stark, it was very stark,
But he got rid of all that weight.
Oh it was stark, you could say it was very stark,
But it made his balls feel all right
That night.

Mike was riding to Belston,
Pulled up for a cup of tea.
Right by the door was a big blonde whore,
She said, "You fancy me?"
Yes he did, yes he did,
Well he fancied a bit.'

Mike drew level with a low, half-timbered estate car whose sleek-haired driver didn't look at him. As the driver was a man, Mike let him go, revved and continued the ballad, remembering a legend he had heard about a cafe on the Great North Road.

'Mike took up a collection
So he could treat his knob.
The drivers threw money in his helmet
And it came to thirty bob,
Yes it did, yes it did,
Well he fancied a bit.

They drove Mike down to a lay-by,
In his arms they laid the blonde,
They got down on a coat between two lorries
And they turned the headlights on,

Yes they did, yes they did,
Well he fancied a bit.

The first time they did it they melted the tar
And it flooded down the Belston Road.
The second time they did it they broke every rule
In the goddam highway code,
Yes they did, yes they did,
Well he fancied a bit.

Wookey Hole and the Albert Memorial,
The Cotswold Hills as well.
He was Stirling Moss and Casanova,
She was Venus and Eskimo Nell,
Yes they were, yes they were,
Well he fancied a bit.

An agent phoned them from London,
He said "I heard you come,
Can I book you for the next seven years
For the London Palladium?
Millions of pounds.
Millions of viewers.
They all fancy a bit."'

Mike would have laughed, but his cock had taken the song too seriously and crouched, ready to spring, compressed by his melodramatic trousers. It talked to him in terse, practical terms. You pick up a hitchhiker and give her a lift as far as Belston, it said. Half-way you stop. She's ugly and smells and says she has the curse, but she tosses you off without chafing. The weight disappears, you can think clearly again and forget about me for a day. Mike told his cock to shut up and pulled into the flinty car park of a warmly lit pub.

The bar was large and square, the woman behind it stubbily built and wide-faced, about fifty, standing below rows of light-bulbs in variously misshapen shades and an anthology of tourist toys – lovebirds on a perch, cardboard mobiles advertising drink, three-cornered flags saying Cornwall and Lancashire, a towering woolly monkey, funny poker-worked notices (God Bless our Mortgaged Home, and Mike imagined the gloombound face of the worker as he produced the two-thousandth copy of that one with his running poker), and postcards, some of which carried bulbous jokes, some of which showed ugly seaside scenes and some of which were pretty.

'Where you headed?' she asked Mike, drawing him a pint and picking two pasties for him with plastic tongs.

'Past Belston,' he said. 'Got to rescue a friend from this terrible woman.'

'Oh yes,' she said, then turned to three men who were sitting at separate tables, but who seemed to be part of the conversation Mike had interrupted. 'Yes, it was thrombosis,' she told them.

'Thrombosis, that's what—'

'Awful.'

'Yes,' she said, 'I didn't know what to do. Gave her a brandy of course—'

'They been married long?'

'Yes, oh yes, oh quite a long time—'

'About seven years, weren't it?'

'Seven? No, much longer than that. I don't know how we got to know them. They used to come in for a drink, then she started to help behind the bar, you know. He used to drink stout, they warned him to stop it because of the thrombosis.'

'He didn't, did he?'

'What, Harry? No. I liked him. Never said much, sort of dry. But he was kind, always remembered the kiddies' birthdays, all that. Never said much.'

'Was he long going?'

'No, very quick. He was very quick. It's the second one too. Only Saturday I heard old Matthew died. Yes.'

The total glumness and its tension made Mike want to laugh. He'd have to if the gloom wasn't dispersed soon. One of the seated men said:

'All got to die some time.'

'Yes,' said the woman. 'It's all the bad buggers live longest.'

'That's why you lived so long,' said the largest of the three men. She leaned over the bar and shook her head.

'Don't you worry. I don't mind dying. Don't mind if I go any day, any minute. Don't you worry.'

'We're not worrying Ellen. Only worrying if you'll leave any money for us.'

'Don't you worry about that either. I've remembered all you lot in my will. Twenty-five pounds I've left you.'

'Twenty-five pounds each.'

'You old nit. Twenty-five pounds between the lot of you for some drinks.'

'We need twenty-five pounds each to get drunk on. On your beer.' The first laugh, from her.

'If you want cheering up, all my old man has to do is get me stuffed and stick me in the corner of the bar. Ah well, all got to die sometime.'

'Yes.'

A crumpled man standing by the door of the Gents' looked up from his brown ale and said:

'That's one thing you can bet on.'

Everyone nodded. The woman said:

'Yes, it's the only thing you can bet on. When you die you're dead.' She seemed very certain and glad of it.

'Yes, you can bet on that.' The woman lowered her voice slightly. 'Yes, I don't believe in God, you see. I don't think there's any such bugger. Pardon me—' (that seemed to be directed at Mike) 'but I don't believe in God, you see. You can't bet on anything.'

The seated men grinned at each other.

One said: 'There's quarter-day, you can bet on that coming round.'

Another said: 'And you can bet on the income-tax man getting you.'

The crumpled man said: 'Now you're getting morbid.'

It was the funniest joke in the world. Mike coughed beer and hung on to his barstool for support. The seated men jogged up and down appreciatively, the woman closed her eyes and let the funny tears roll, the crumpled man repeated the gag as he stepped up for a refill. Mike had the happy feeling that the whole conversation had been a deliberate build-up towards a punch-line, a performance not laid on for his benefit but for the pleasure of anyone in the world wise enough to be in this dopey bar and nowhere else. They liked the way he laughed. Wiping her eyes, the woman announced:

'This young man's off to rescue his mate from some woman.'

'Bloody hell,' said the largest man. 'I wish he'd do that for this little lot.'

'He's getting noosed then, your mate?'

'Man and woman, there's nothing like man and woman,' said the woman. Everyone said ho ho. 'There's nothing like it if the man's not a bugger and the woman's not a bitch—'

'As St Paul reminds us,' said the crumpled man. 'But Blake said:

He who binds to himself a Joy
Doth the winged life destroy;
But he who kisses the Joy as it flies
Lives in Eternity's sunrise.'

He straightened his long back as he recited, then grinned and relaxed again.

'That Blake sounds like all the rest of you,' said the woman.

'So he was,' said the crumpled man. 'But he had stronger guts and bigger eyes. But what's this young man? Is he like Blake?'

'I want to be,' said Mike. 'I mean I want to write anyway. Pamphlets and things.'

The crumpled man nodded, a signal to continue.

'No, I want to write about war, against cruelty. About all the crap which people take. About the way the rich still run the country and still own the bloody country because we're mostly half-asleep. About the law which no one understands except the lawyers, the whole legal system which looks to me designed to protect property more than people. And things like that—'

Mike was stumbling, couldn't explain what he hadn't written and there was a silence lasting two seconds before the crumpled man bought him a beer, shook his hand and conducted an hour-long seminar on Spence, Cobbett and Paine. By the end of it Mike's head was whirling with revolution, the uncanny feeling that he had fallen happily into a nest of surviving Chartists, and when he clumped out, to shouts of 'Mind how you go, son,' he was drunk with hope. Good people.

Remounting his bike, he let his head bend backwards loosely and stared at the sky. It was going to be easy. He would talk Jack into leaving and if Lorna tried to get in his way, well he'd talk her out of the way. The politician in his head started summing up the pub. A useful experience. Bloody hell. Mike kicked the politician several times around his brain, then started the engine.

Mike stopped twice more on his way to the Hall, both times to rest his eyes, bruised by headlights. He began to hate the road; the pub behind him, safe, populated by unthreatening strangers, had been hard to leave. Now in his mind he saw no white or dark girl, no honey throbber, he saw only the massive Hall, sometimes a construction of perfect white stones, sometimes a temple carved out of one black rock.

As it veered down the drive, Mike's machine threw a wake of small stones towards the moon. The building's front face was chequered with large square lights and as the engine snarled and stopped, Rodney appeared on the long stone balcony, a fat white king in a dressing-gown woven of gold. As Mike hinged off his crash helmet and pushed back his goggles, Rodney waved and smiled.

'Good to see you, good to see you. What brings you here?'

Rodney tried to prevent the question from sounding anything but a pleasantry, but he misjudged it, there was fear on his breath, he was nearly stumbling with whisky, leaning on the balustrade too heavily. His head wobbled on his neck. Mike put his gloved fists on his hips and shouted up:

'Got something to tell you.'

'Come up and tell me. The front door's open.'

'I'm not coming in. You come out here, I'll tell you.'

'But what's it about?'

'It might shatter you. You might fall to pieces and the bits might float all over the park. Come down. I'll tell you.'

Mike didn't move. Stared upwards, permanent as a statue. Clenching his jaw, Rodney moved through the soft bedroom, down the wide, glowing stairway. At the front door he paused and looked once more at Mike. Rodney walked out on to the front steps, feeling like a victim in a foreign country who has lived as best he can without knowing which of his actions are crimes, without knowing how he may be punished. Only the redness of Mike's eyes, which suggested that he might be a brother drunk, encouraged Rodney.

Mike said: 'Where's Lorna?'

'She's away for the weekend.'

It was a lie. Lorna had taken advantage of the full moon to go night-shooting. Somewhere on the estate she was riding Masterman II, picking off badgers, water-rats, anything that moved. Rodney was never asked to go shooting with her. She brought home the corpses in a bag and lugged them down to the cellar herself.

'Kick your lousy job,' said Mike.

'What's wrong with Global Image?'

'You don't know? Then we'd better talk about it, find out. What's your particular job?'

'Mike, I'd rather tell you than anyone, but it's confidential. Anyway, you might misunderstand.'

'Let me tell you. Just let me tell you. Your job is to read the newspapers and help monitor TV and radio? And whenever you find a derogatory reference to West Germany, you clip it, right?'

'I can't talk about it.'

'Or for that matter any reference to Nazi Germany, right? When there's a new book about the Nazis, you read it pretty thoroughly, don't you? You report on the book. What's more, you report on the author, right? Is he a Red, is he a liberal or is he – all right? Is he stirring it up? Or is he burying it?'

'I'm not standing interrogation, Mike—'

'Rodney, I'm not asking you questions, I'm telling you. You're being used—'

'Damn that, you're being used is a joke. You're the one who's being used – by the Reds and the queers and the bloody Trots and the anarchists and anyone who comes to you with a CND badge and a hole in their shoes, any bloody subversive can get you and use you—'

'Yes, I know about that, I just wish I was more useful to them. I know when I'm being used, and if it suits me I let it happen. OK, I'm used by subversives on the left, well, I'm a subversive on the left so that's all right. But you don't even know who's using you. You reckon Global Image gets its budget for boosting the German tourist trade? You reckon? You want to look through the balance sheets in that bloody office of yours. I've got photostats at home if you ever want to look at them. Soon after you file a report on a newspaper article, that newspaper begins to get a crop of pro-German letters, intelligent letters they seem, excusing letters, hints that Hitler had some positive qualities, hints that the Russians had some Belsens of their own, hints that Belsen was exaggerated, that Belsen never existed, that Belsen was a health resort.'

'It doesn't work like that.'

'You bugger, you know how it works.' Mike gulped for air twice. 'Then tell me this, tell me this, who owns it? Some holding company? And who owns the holding company? Lorna's got some shares in it. Who else? German industrialists, John Birchers, British fascists?'

'I don't know, I don't know that. Mike, I'm not lying to you, I don't know where the money comes from.'

'Who owns you, Rodney? Who the hell owns you? I'm not playing any games, I'm going to put a bomb under that firm in the next two months. They took you for a ride, mate. Jump off.'

'You know I can't, it's going too fast, you know I can't pull out even if I wanted to. You reckon they'd let me, well, you don't know them. But I'll tell you something, I don't want to pull out. You big black leather cowboy, you black bloody knight—' he began to march down the steps – 'I've got a good life with Lorna, there'll be no bombs under it. It's good. I have a good time. Friend. You've been my friend, you called yourself that and as soon as I begin winning and you begin losing you snap at me, you talk big soft phrases out of your big soft pink cloud. One day you'll grow up and find yourself leaning on a pink cloud, then you'll fall a thousand feet. You'll be such a mess nobody'll want to bury the pieces. Clown in the clouds.'

'Oh, get the poet of the upper middle class, get him.'

'Class? I never said anything about class.'

'Of course you didn't, it's a word to waken the dead. If the dead woke up, they'd talk about class, bet on it. Class killed a lot of them. There's an upper-middle-class way to be conceived and an upper-middle-class way to be buried. Try and live classlessly in England and see what happens. What has no class in this country?'

For an answer Rodney picked up a stone, looked at it with a grin and threw it. It hit Mike's shin and bounced among the gravel. Mike picked it up.

'There's a good answer. A stone. This stone you chose, lying in the driveway of the Munche mansion, belongs without dispute to the owner of this mansion. To Lorna. In revolutions the skies of towns are filled with cobblestones. Among all the fenced and barbed-wire fields of green England there's not one stone without an owner. Every man who owns as much as a long thin garden, its plants smoked black by trains, owns more stones than he can ever count. But most people don't ever own even one stone. Stone-owners don't have much choice; they need, from the day they start to own, more stones than the earth can serve them with. But for the stoneless, there's a choice. A man without stones can either fight outnumbering statistics and climb the wall topped with broken wine bottles to join the stone-owners. Or he can join the stoneless like me who think that stones should belong to everyone.'

Still laughing, Rodney answered: 'They don't even know how to treat a stone. They wouldn't know how. A good property man, though, a good property man knows his own stones, he watches over their unmoving flocks. The good stoneherd, the Good Stoneherds, they *own*, they are *responsible*, they love their own stones, organize them into great rivers like this drive, hew them into houses like this, well have them hewn, have them carved into noble statues; they love their stones, they do, they become, by their care for their own, like gods.'

Above Rodney's laughter, Mike heard a roar, the roar of a sickened throat. Then another. Then another.

Rodney said: 'It's nothing.'

Mike walked past him and in through the front door, paused to locate the roaring and slowly unbolted the door leading down to the cellar. The roaring stopped. Mike trembled terribly, as if every part of his skin were effervescent, as if a very slight electric current were on the run through his bloodstream. The door wouldn't open, so he leaned his right ear against its black surface. Slow footsteps. Mike folded his hand and began to drum, louder and louder. More footsteps, then someone was leaning against the far side of the door. A tired voice said: 'Lor-na, Lor-na.'

'Who's that? Is that Jack? Listen, listen, this is Mike. Can you come out of there?'

'You're not Mike. Mike's dead.'

'Jack.' Silence. 'Jack. I know you. This is Mike.'

The two bolts inside the door, well-oiled, moved back, silently but for the final clicks. Mike pushed the door and it opened a few inches; a chain prevented it from opening further. He could see yellow light on the white-washed stone ceiling inside, the beginning of those concrete steps but not the end of them, the toe of one polished boot, an army boot, polished to army standards.

Jack began to talk through the gap: 'I know you're dead, Mike. You're not Mike. Mike's dead. Made himself dead. They call, they call it suicide, they call it, while the bal-ance of the mind, the bal-ance was disturbed.' Jack's shadows swayed to the rhythm of his words. 'Mike did that, he went strange because his mind went strange. Things got into his mind and poison, pus got into his mind. He went all strange. Tried, he tried yes he tried to be Mike, but he, he, he got – tired. No, not – tired, he got poison. In the brain. And this is how it started. Mike saw the Colonel. Saw him. And Mike, Mike hated. He, er, made the Colonel die. Made him die. Mike did that. And then, then, he was glad, and then, then, he got very pleased, very glad, he hated, hated, hated Lor-na. And he – hated me because he hated Lorna and he hated. He was, he was once Mike, but then he hated everyone and he went all Judas striking out kissing and killing kissing and killing kissing and killing and talking, because he learned to talk to people, talking, talking, a trumpet of pus out of his mouth, all be slaves, we'll all be slaves, the first ones, when the Reds come in, he wanted slaves too, he'd betray slaves, Judas, sick Mike, and he wanted all the torturers to come into England and torture to start for everyone in the suburbs, towns, everyone, torture ships full of torturers up to the beaches, torturers dropping out of the sky. But he couldn't. Small, sick Mike. He couldn't betray everyone. No. He couldn't.

Too small, too sick. They knew, we knew, Lorna knew, Lorna saw Judas, she saw him, she knew that kiss, acid kiss. So Mike had to kill himself, he shot himself with a gun, his head was a bad mess. He did it on a couch, he did, looking, he was looking at dirty books, dirty pictures while he did it. Shot. Dead. But Lorna took Jack, to save him. Saved me. Showed me. And this is the cellar.' He was shouting, his voice ascending. 'When it drops, now listen, now listen, when it drops: first the whole damn sky will go like blood. Then the whole damn sky will go white, white like the sun. Then it will be full of hurricanes on fire. Every bit in the sky will, every bit of the sky will slap down. Bird bones all black. Melted aeroplanes. Clouds burn. That's the sky, just the sky, that's just the sky. The seas, ask me, the sea, yes, the sea'll get tall and stamp around the world, making fizzing, boiling, making fizzing boiling noises. Fish frying, white bellies up. Submarines frying, white bellies up. The world with its white belly up. One day the sea stops fizzing and boiling, it stops that and goes still, rests. And that day the sea turns bad. Bad sea rushing into all the great cracks in the land. The earth, the land, you care about that. Yes. You care about that, you'll probably be on that bit yourself. Continents burn, yes, the continents burn and curl up like newspapers. Islands sink, sink, sink into the bad sea. All the colours on the map, all the atlas colours, red England, yellow Russia, green America, oh patchwork Africa, all of 'em – just black. Black. Listen. Now this, you're holding the door, this is the safe cellar. Salvation cellar. You see. Can be here, and safe, it's safe as we can. Me, Lorna, we can do it. Me, Lorna, Rodney.'

Mike turned his face for an instant to Rodney, and while Jack stormed on about the safety of the cellar, Rodney, leaning against the panelled wall, chattered: 'Mike, we didn't give him this, we didn't teach him this. He was scared, we tried to help, nobody told him you were dead, we didn't do that, what would anyone want to say that for, we didn't. He was so scared, he's mad, you can hear that for yourself, it was to save him from the nuthouse, he was so scared, he was terrified about the bomb, but, you know, he was just as terrified of the nuthouse. So we let him build, Lorna had him build this shelter so that he'd find a sort of comfort. Protection. Comfort.'

'Make him open the door.'

'He's dangerous. Honestly, Mike, it's not safe. He's, he's possessive about the shelter – about the cellar. Thinks he's got to guard it.'

Mike screamed: 'I'll see for myself what he thinks. I'll find out who made him think it.' He caught Rodney by the lapels of his dressing-gown and dragged him to the door. He tugged suddenly so that Rodney's head nodded. Rodney said: 'Jack. This is Rodney. It's time to open the door. This is Mike here with me. Mike's not dead.' Mike shook him, staring into his eyes. 'Mike hasn't betrayed anyone. You must talk to him. Open the door. Lorna wants you to open the door.'

A pause, then the chain dangled and Jack stood there. Mike had half expected a bearded, robed figure in manacles. But Jack's red hair was cropped to near-stubble, his chin was newly shaven, his long hands were clean. The khaki uniform he wore was sharply pressed, each button intricately polished, the belt exactly blancoed. His face was made of glossy white paper. His good eye lay deep. The cheekbones and the concave cheeks were like wings. His whole skull, it seemed, was thinly clothed, and at his neck the skin hung in two vertical folds. His head seemed to have taken on a different shape, as if some parts of the brain had developed massively while other parts had withered.

Mike swallowed and swallowed again, preventing himself from vomiting. Jack swayed with the weight of the chains of drugs, closing his eye against Mike, wincing back against the stone wall, muttering: 'Lies, lies, the liars.' Mike put out his arms, Jack opened his eye, half smiled, at the same time rolling his head as if avoiding many blows, and then embraced Mike.

'See my cellar. See it, please.'

'Jack, I've got to get you away, quick.'

'Yes, yes. But—' he managed the name, '—Mike, Mike, Mike. Huh? See my cellar.'

'Jack, we've got to—'

'Please, Mike. I worked years. See it. I can't explain what happened. Have to show you my cellar.'

With one of Jack's arms round his shoulders, Mike followed the stone steps down, round a right-angle and up to a door painted white. The door was thick, painted exactly, obsessively, as if with the brush from a child's paintbox. It had no handle, but Jack leaned forward and it swung open on its central pivot. They walked into a cube of darkness. Even when Jack switched on the light it was hard to focus the shape of the room, for it was paved, walled and ceilinged with black tiles, only relieved by a chromium plug in the square depression in the floor and the shining shower fitment directly over it.

'Cleansing, it's the cleanser room,' said Jack. 'We got this big water-tank.'

'An underground tank?'

'Underground, surrounded by lead, all cased in lead, safe as houses.'

Jack laughed. He pushed open another door faced with black tiles and they were in the second, much larger chamber, a room shaped something like a duck seen in profile. They entered through the head and neck of the duck, treading immediately on durable carpet, passing on their left-hand side an embroidered curtain hanging from the ceiling. Its faded needlework showed ambiguous religious scenes. A man who might have been a martyr or an infidel kneeling as a giant raised a massive sword. Two men lowering a third, with ropes, into a hole in the ground, or they might be lifting him out. Men on all fours under a sky full of falling objects, either sharp rain or manna.

'Art treasures behind the curtain,' said Jack, swishing a gap in it, showing for a few seconds great packing cases, canvases in sacks and suitcases held together with leather straps.

Mike was already turning away, looking down the room towards the plain white curtain opposite, letting his eyes run along the stones of the old vaulted ceiling. Each eccentrically set stone had been painted carefully, individually, each in a different shade of red, varying from creamy pink to a ferocious vermilion.

'Took a month, two months to get that ceiling right,' said Jack.

At first the chamber appeared to centre on an oval dining-table, perfectly polished, ancient. At one end was a tapestried chair, its legs curving, ending in brown claws. There were two other chairs, one with a padded plastic seat and back, the other a plain wood kitchen chair which had been painted black. But the true centre of the room was the large wooden globe which depended from the ceiling on golden chains. On the globe continents and islands stood out in wooden relief and each country was painted in its own colour.

Beyond it, on the far wall, hung a reproduction of Dali's mid-air crucifixion, Jesus flying away on his primitive aeroplane cross. For a second Mike's mind showed Lorna crucified, her wounds radiation burns, zooming away from an irradiated world and returning to rule the ashes. Mike dismissed the picture, examining the cultural apparatus around the painting – battery radio and battery record player, bookcases full of new and de luxe volumes. He picked out an oddly bound book. It was two years' worth of the *Tatler*.

'Bound some of those, I did,' said Jack. He sat himself in the black chair and closed his eyes. Mike looked at more titles: what could Lorna allow to survive into her new civilization? Debrett, Surtees, *Punch* of course, Tennyson, the Bible, sure, a file of *Daily Telegraph*s, Kipling, Waugh, Virgil, Churchill, *The Whip and the Rod*, *Bulldog Drummond*, *Nordenholt's Million*, Fleming, Foxe's *Book of Martyrs*, Herman Kahn and Ayn Rand bound in prayerbook style. There were also do-it-yourself manuals covering the theory and practice of car-building, chemistry, Christianity, physics, freemasonry, the stock market, health, cookery, botany, medicine, meteorology. After it fell, Lorna, Rodney and Jack could bustle around the cellar acting out a typical day at the London Stock Exchange. There were far fewer records – Wagners, musicals, Pat Boone. Until he turned to Jack again, now sitting upright, left arm holding his right wrist tight behind the back of the black chair, Mike went through a minor upheaval of laughter. But Jack was there, real, Jack hollowed out to produce a shelter for Lorna, a shelter which might simply be a murderous joke on Jack. Mike walked over and pulled back the white curtain, exposing a small supermarket. There stood three tall alleys of food, carefully arranged on their plastic shelves. As he sidled past breakfast cereals and into the fruit-juice area, Mike noticed that each packet and tin had been marked with its current price. Presumably the survivors would be paid wages which they would be able to spend in this buried shop. Other labels showed the nutritive value of each food, while at the end of the first food corridor was a file which catalogued the entire contents of the cellar. The second and third alleys were also packed with bright cans and each of them led to a deep-freezer, apparently worked by Calor gas.

Now Jack was on his feet, long hands pushing downwards at the cloth of his trouserlegs, staring at the ground. His head jerked, 'It's time, Mike. Can you get me some?'

'Some what? What do you need?'

'Don't know. You must know. Get me some. Lorna gives it, she gives it to me.'

'Is it an injection?'

Jack swayed his head from side to side, smiling painfully. 'It's pills, you know, pills and a kind of drink, liquid drink, don't know what it is.'

'Jack, I haven't got any here, whatever it is. Maybe we can find it outside if you'll come now.'

Jack began to beat his thighs. 'Need it, need it.'

'I'll get you something, some sort of a drink anyway. If you'll come out.'

'My throat's all sand and – dust. Some sort of drink – would help.'

Mike clicked open the fridge and pulled out a beer can. He held it for a second as it passed through his mind that it was about half as heavy as a hand grenade. It fitted his hand comfortably, frigidly. From a drawer he unjumbled a two-legged tin-opener from a tangle of metal cutlery, punched a slit in the can's top and the foam spurted, making a triangle on the tin's top and several chill white spots over the back of his hand, spots which almost immediately became transparent. The second slit, on the opposite edge of the can, produced only a dribble of foam. He held the can to the mouth of a heavy cylindrical glass, tilting glass and can together until they formed a right-angle. Jack did not touch the glass as it stood on the white table. Instead he pushed up his chair, crouched forward from it and put his ear to the top of the glass. 'It crackles,' he said. 'Sizzles like a log in the fire.' He sniffed the sick smell of the foam, but then, through the side of the glass, he began to stare farther and farther into the depths of the beer, his head approaching the circular glass wall as near as his eyes could focus. The foam became milkier, less brittle, softer, almost sagging. His eyes drank. Bubbles rose, often apparently from nothing but the thick bottom of the glass, sometimes mass movements in currents, in columns. Sometimes singly. One by one they plinked and bounced against the golden underside of the foam-scum. That underside was a mass of gold ball-bearings. A few obstinate larger bubbles adhered to the inner walls, but as Jack watched them, they also, one by one, detached themselves and flew upwards, apparently moving at the pace of a running man. Jack sipped at the glass, his upper lip passing through the layer of foam. Then he returned to his observations.

The bubbles still rose at the same speed. Holding the glass up and staring once more at the underside of the foam, Jack pushed his right forefinger slowly through the foam so that it emerged in the gold drink, pressing through the cloud, stretching the cloud, his rounded fingertip decorated with bubbles. He noticed a minimal black object dive to the bottom of the glass, trailing bubbles about half its own size. Dust or a fly-turd maybe. The empty quarter of the glass, filled only with air and lined with polar patterns of foam, looked bleak and frightening. But the depths. Jack tried to imagine the fish that might inhabit such a shining pillar of liquid, but each time he tried to imagine fish, of whatever exotic colour scheme, they turned over on their backs and floated up into the foam. He tried to concentrate on the perfection of a single bubble, but it rocketed upwards and turned to foam. It was cold, but it looked warm.

A minute later Mike said: 'What do you see in there?'

'Many dead.' Jack was crying. 'I'd like to live in there. All my life. That's a beautiful place.' He grabbed the glass and Mike took half a step back, afraid he was going to throw it because his visions had been broken. But Jack gulped down the beer and smiled. Mike found himself calculating – if Jack could use the word life, and say it with such affection at such a bad moment when he needed his drug and couldn't get it, maybe Jack could live.

There were three more doors in the room. One led to a cupboard-size lavatory.

The second door led to a fur-covered floor, a great bed, a triangular dressing-table, a grained wardrobe – a perfect reproduction of Lorna's bedroom upstairs, only marred by the fact that a portrait of the Colonel hung where there should have been a window. Mike backed out.

The third door, dull khaki with two bolts on the outside. Jack said: 'She kept me in there. She – you see, if I didn't do the right things or I was what she thought bad, you see, bad, she kept me in there.' It was a cell. Shit-colour, a hole in the floor for a bog, an Army bed with biscuit mattresses, a dun locker, tin basin and the bell of a huge loudspeaker sticking out of the wall. The only decoration, pasted on the paint of the wall, were chinny girls in 1942 bathing-dresses, soft-focus nudes from Lilliput and hard-focus pictures of atrocities. Opposite the bed stood a plain, scarred workbench, neatly arrayed with tools. There was a pile of several hundred small wooden crosses. As Mike picked up one after another, observing how carefully they had been sandpapered, Jack gave a small, resigned gesture.

'I was working on those. For after. For after. I was – meant to put names on them but I didn't want to.' He lay on the bed. 'Mike. You don't, I mean, you don't want to stay and – help us? You wouldn't stay? I thought you wouldn't.'

'Do you want to stay?'

'I don't know. I don't want anything.'

'Don't you want to be free?'

'Never been free. Have you been there?'

'I've never never been somewhere where someone else dictates what I do, what I eat, when I sleep, my whole life, where someone takes my mind and makes it into whatever shape pleases them.'

'Well, you're bloody lucky then.'

'We're getting out now.'

'Mike, I'm tired you see. She gives me – I'm tired you see. I'll tell you. I'm scared to go out.'

'Doesn't she scare you more? You're getting out now, with me.'

He tried to pull Jack by the arm, but the arm was limp. Mike turned, inspired, to the workbench, grabbed a heavy chisel in his left hand, a mallet in his right. Behind Jack's head was the dull grey corner of the enormous water-tank. The chisel jabbed through. Jack did not move until the head of the fountain leaped into the room and the water darkened half his uniform. By the time both men were through the door and into the shower vestibule, the biscuit mattresses had been blown across the floor by the water. By the time Jack and Mike reached the head of the stairs, the water was flooding across the carpet of the large chamber, was beginning to wash against the bottom shelf of the bookcase.

Rodney lay in the hall, moaning something, out of his mind with Scotch. Mike went through his pockets and took not only the keys of Rodney's car but six pounds seven shillings in cash. With Jack he stepped out of the front door.

There, in the spotlight of the moon, half-way between the car and the motorbike, stood Masterman II and on him Lorna. In the crook of her right arm she was holding, lightly, a rifle. Mike pushed Jack in front of him as they ran towards the corner of the house, then grabbed him round the shoulders and forced him onwards so that they both fell together when Mike tripped on a croquet hoop. Mike swore, using Lorna's name to swear with, the dirtiest word he knew, Lorna and Masterman II and the rifle moved nearer. Pointblank range. Mike's right arm circled on the grass like a compass while he watched Lorna's blank face. His arm circled again, retraced a few inches and then his hand closed on a croquet ball. Lorna was about to speak. Mike had added up the chances. The rifle was for him. Lorna's words would be for Jack, words which would sink swiftly to the quick of his brain. Before Lorna could begin Mike aimed the ball at her mouth and let it go, a blue ball, arcing towards her, falling short and thumping her horse in the flank. The horse reared violently and Lorna fell, elbow and thigh on the gravel. Mike was beside her, armed with a croquet mallet, before she could raise her rifle higher than her knee. He pulled the gun away from her and, as she stepped backwards, levelled it at her head. He heard Jack approach him slowly, then pass him, then approach him, and lie down on the gravel to weep great waves.

'Into your bloody house,' Mike said. 'Don't look at him or I'll shoot you. Don't talk or I'll blast you. Nothing. Go back and play with your bloody Rodney. Keep out of our bloody way.'

She laughed. But she walked back to the Hall, shutting the front door behind her. She stepped over Rodney.

Mike levered Jack into the back of Rodney's car. As they travelled down the drive they heard a long wail. Lorna had climbed to the roof of the Hall and was cranking the air-raid siren, laughing to herself. She knew Jack was beyond reasonable hope. Mike knew also that Jack was beyond the sort of ordinary small hope that has logical limits. By those standards he was an animal. Maybe a tiger grafted with the fur of a mouse, all its teeth extracted without anaesthetic. A tuskless dwarf elephant. A bird which has spent a year amassing dust among its feathers in a box, a mad bird. He belonged to a mental home, maybe, some white and disinfected human zoo. It would be kinder, any sentimentalist would tell you. But Mike was cruel. He took Jack out into the world.

V £1

Thomas Pynchon

'The book sails with majesty through caverns measureless to man. Few books haunt the waking or sleeping mind, but this is one'
Time

This is the first novel by the author of *Gravity's Rainbow*, and a profoundly impressive and original work in its own right. The search for the mysterious V ranges from New York to Cairo to Alexandria to Malta. Apart from its strange heroine, the book's characters include sailors, spies, priests, philosophers, bums and bawds.

'This work may well stand as one of the very best novels of the century'
Atlantic Review

'Brilliant and turbulent . . . staggering promise'
New York Times

'If Mack Sennett, Nathaniel West and Mike Todd had collaborated to stage the Worlds' Greatest Vaudeville they might have produced something like Pynchon's novel'
Boston Sunday Globe

Also by Pynchon in Picador: *Gravity's Rainbow*